TALES FROM THE Front Porch Swing

IRIS VANDEVENTER-WHITNEY

Editing and Design Services by Christian Writing Services
www.ChristianWritingServices.com.
Cover design and typesetting by Shannon Herring
(Shannon@ChristianWritingServices.com).
Copy Editing by Karen Burkett (Karen@ChristianWritingServices.com).

Printed in the United States of America

ISBN 978-0-9825111-2-1

To all the precious people who strive to make
a difference in someone else's life.
Like Mrs. Thomas, they may be far from perfect,
but they work daily to help others.

To every reader--may God bless you as you enter
the world of Mrs. Thomas.

Contents

Chapter 1

Mrs. Anna Thomas sat on the front porch swing. Tall and thin, she was nevertheless sturdy as a young Amish girl. Her bangs were curled about her forehead—the rest of her dark hair pulled tightly back in a twist. She was wearing a plain dress covered by an ever-present apron. Slowly rocking back and forth, she thought about the roomers who often sat on the swing with her and confided their life stories and, at times, their secrets.

She certainly did not want to probe into their personal lives. She listened to the boarders tell their stories and encouraged them when she felt they were faltering. Mrs. Thomas thought she had a "calling" to listen to others unload their fears and hurts and to help them if need be. It was her duty.

Others might not see her duty this way. But wasn't she the one with the calling? Well, Mrs. Thomas was not about to waste her time worrying about what others thought. People just didn't understand these special callings!

She made it a rule not to interfere or force her opinion on others. However, it was necessary at times, Mrs. Thomas mused. *My land, how could I have refused to advise that little gal Lela? It was a neighborly and kind thing to do.*

She thought about the young women who had passed through her rooming house. *Goodness, have there been twenty-five or thirty?* Ten years ago, she had opened her home to others. She not only enjoyed a comfortable income but also felt blessed with a family of sorts. Her current "family" consisted of Hattie, Elma, Kate, and Mandy Jayne.

The young women helped make up for the years of loneliness she had experienced during her early years. *All right, Anna. Don't get yourself upset. You need to get up and start supper for the ladies—they will be gathering soon.*

Jumping up from the swing, she made her way into the house, silently reminding herself to have the town's handyman out to fix the squeaky screen door. *I remember how that squeaking used to bother Lela. I told her I would get it fixed—somehow, I never got around to it. Now Hattie cringes at the squeaking. Personally, I think it's a homey sound. I like it.*

Mrs. Thomas's mind returned to thoughts of her former boarder, and she wondered how Lela and her new husband were doing. When Lela first lived at the boardinghouse, Mrs. Thomas didn't dream she was divorced and had two little girls. All the time they sat and talked on the swing she had no clue Lela held such a secret. Mrs. Thomas decided everyone must have a "secret box."

She chuckled when she realized how long ago it was that Lela roomed there. *Goodness, it's been five years now, and her husband is hardly new anymore.* She hoped Lela was happy after the heartbreak she suffered that horrible summer. Just thinking about it caused her Mrs. Thomas's eyes to tear.

Jogging her thoughts back to the present, Mrs. Thomas followed the smell of newly baked bread into the kitchen. There on the table sat four beautiful loaves of crusty-topped bread and two pans of yeast rolls she had baked earlier in the day. What a sight and what a smell!

She knew she should wait but yearned to swath a roll with butter and eat it. And so she did. Licking the last crumbs from her lips, Mrs. Thomas reluctantly pushed herself away from the table and began to prepare supper for her "family of sorts."

Mrs. Thomas jolted as screams broke the silence. *Now what?* she thought as she hurried to the source of the racket. There in the front parlor, standing on the settee, was Hattie. Usually so prim and neat, she was now a tumbled picture of hysteria. Her loosely styled hair was hanging in her face and she was emitting shrieks of "eek, eek" to high heaven.

Elma, a pretty dark-haired girl, had arrived on the scene and was searching for the cause of the commotion. Mrs. Thomas stood there with her mouth hanging open as she took in the scene. Elma came from behind the settee holding a small snake by the tail. It flexed its body in a futile attempt to gain freedom, sending Hattie into another chorus of "eeks." She tried to climb onto the back of settee to distance herself from the snake.

"Oh, Hattie, it's only a garter snake, and it won't hurt you— or anything else, for that matter," Elma hollered over her shoulder as she headed for the back door. Opening the screen door, she heaved the snake across the yard and watched it slither away into the garden.

Hattie, visibly shaken, stepped down from the settee and headed up to her room. Elma shook her head as she watched Hattie climb the stairs. "Why she carries on so is beyond me. I would be more afraid of the fellow she's stuck on. Oh well, it's none of my business."

"That's exactly what I was thinking," responded Mrs. Thomas. Elma gave her a black look and disappeared out the screen door.

The door slammed behind Elma and Mrs. Thomas returned to the kitchen to finish the meal. She thought, *It will be tense at the supper table tonight. The remark Elma made about Hattie's friend was not at all necessary. Why, I wouldn't butt into anyone's business like that for the life of me!*

Kate and Mandy Jayne entered the dining room with Elma trailing behind. Kate was shorter than Elma and Hattie. She had a gentle manner complemented by fair hair, a sweet face, and soft voice. Mandy Jayne, on the other hand, had a pretty face and exceptionally beautiful teeth, but was a bit spoiled and sharp-tongued.

Seeing no sign of Hattie, Mrs. Thomas walked to the stairs to call her for supper. A few minutes later, Hattie came dragging into the dining room, her eyes red and swollen. Mrs. Thomas rushed to divert attention from her and avoid unwelcome questions from the others.

"Ladies, did I tell you how I prevented trouble down at the mill today?" Mrs. Thomas eyed the women to see if her ruse worked. She seemed to have their attention. "Well, here's the way I saved the day for two mill workers . . ."

Elma jumped up and headed for the front porch. Falling into the swing, she considered what to do next. One thing she did not want to do was listen to one more story from Mrs. Thomas. If that meant going to bed with no supper, so be it. *Hmmm, I know what I'll do. I'll raid the kitchen after everyone else goes to bed.* Her spirits lifted, and she hurried into town.

Meanwhile, in the dining room Mrs. Thomas tried once more. "I will continue my story now that things have settled." Hattie gave no notice, while Kate and Mandy Jayne eyed each other with knowing smiles. "I was about to the mill when I heard a loud noise—a swooshin' sound—and I thought I saw smoke.

But it wasn't smoke; it was . . ." She didn't finish her sentence because of Hattie's quick departure from the table.

"Now what in the world has got into that gal? I declare, I never saw such a bunch of skittish ladies! It appears it will just be the three of us for supper," she commented to Kate and Mandy. But they were busy eating, their eyes glued to their plates.

"I have a special treat tonight—looks as if there will be plenty for all. I have strawberries with rich whipped cream, all on top of a warm flaky biscuit. I know they are delicious because I tasted one to make sure they were good!"

The ladies giggled as they eyed the pan and saw how many strawberries and biscuits were missing. However, they made no comment and finished the meal in silence.

After dinner Mrs. Thomas tidied up the kitchen and thought, *This was an unusual day, all around!* She soon discovered the day's turmoil wasn't finished.

Elma returned home from town. Her face was distorted with anger. With tightly clenched jaws and hands squeezed into fists, she marched up to her room. Before Elma reached her room, Mrs. Thomas called up the stairway asking if something was wrong. Elma didn't say a word.

Mrs. Thomas waited a short time and then slipped quietly up to Elma's room to tell her she had strawberries and biscuits saved for her. She knocked softly on the door, not knowing what to expect.

The door jerked opened and Elma stood in the doorway glaring at Mrs. Thomas. Her voice exploded, "Don't you think I might want some privacy? If I wanted to talk, I would have stayed downstairs." With that, Elma slammed the door.

Shocked, Mrs. Thomas didn't know how to react. She turned quickly and hurried down the stairs. Her face carried the frightened look of someone fleeing from an attack.

Aching for the peace and comfort of her swing, Mrs. Thomas headed for the front porch. She collapsed on the swing and forced herself to lean back, trying to relax. It was wasted effort, however. Her hands clung to the swing with a white-knuckle grasp, and she rocked it much more aggressively than usual. Tears drifted down her cheeks. She didn't know she was crying until her tears dripped one by one onto her bodice.

Tension mounted inside her until she leaped from the swing and bolted down the lane, all the while crying, "What have I done that Elma should treat me that way?" Blinded by tears, she could barely see her way.

Suddenly she veered from the path and turned into the wooded area, stumbling to a favorite spot deep inside the woods. A fallen tree offered a perfect place to sit, but Mrs. Thomas fell into the thick grass and laid her face on a log naked of the tree's bark. She welcomed the cool compress it provided her swollen face.

She knew not, and she cared not, how long she tarried there. Nor was she aware of the evening's dampness that covered her like a blanket.

Without warning, a voice bellowed, "Annie, Annie, can you hear me? I've come for you." A frantic barking burst the air and then Elmo's voice asked, "Did you find her, Trix? Show me where she is."

Mrs. Thomas stirred when she felt a warm tongue furiously licking her cheeks. She uttered a cry and threw her arms about Trix's neck. She held on tight for fear if she loosened her grip, Trix would leave her. Trix was not a special dog to look at. A non-descript mixed breed, he was not a big dog—just a medium size—and sported short brindled fur. Though his looks were not special, he was special indeed. One could never find more love or loyalty in a dog.

Mrs. Thomas heard Elmo's voice, and there he was. "Oh Elmo, how did you find me? This is my special place in the woods."

"Annie, this is no longer yours alone. Trix is the one who found you, and he will never forget this spot." Elmo gave a mischievous smile and remarked, "Of course, he won't tell anyone."

Mrs. Thomas, weak and shaky, looked up at Elmo. Six feet tall with dark hair and a burly build, he always spoke in a loud voice. But now his voice was oh so soft and gentle. She held tightly to his arm while he helped her up. He sensed her weakness and suggested she sit on the fallen tree. "Old Trix will stay with you while I go get the wagon to transport you home."

"Elmo, I think I can make it if I go slow and hang on to you. I'm sorry to be so much trouble. There is only so much one can stand, and I've reached the 'so much' mark!"

They trudged toward the boardinghouse. After a time of comfortable silence, Mrs. Thomas said, "Elmo, there are things I just don't understand. I've been reading that Bible I found in the attic, and I'm trying to follow what it says to do. Yet, I've had more trouble lately than I had before I started reading it. Why?"

"There are some things, Annie, we can't understand and may never understand. But if you follow what it says, you must also believe it, or there is no value in it for you. I have little knowledge of the Bible, as you know. I'm just speaking plain common sense!"

"You've got common sense, Elmo, and that's for sure. I did read in a verse this morning that we would have hard times. It had to do with refining us and making us strong. I'm not sure I care for this refining business!"

Elmo threw back his head and the roar of his laughter filled the air. Annie was something else—that was for sure!

They reached the house with no further conversation. Mrs. Thomas sat thankfully on the swing, and Elmo joined her. Trix made himself comfortable, curling up on top of Mrs. Thomas's feet. To look at the three, one would never dream there was a problem.

At that moment, the screen door flew open and Elma came rushing out. Tears poured from her red and swollen eyes. She sank down on the top porch step and buried her face in her hands. Sobbing, she tried to tell Mrs. Thomas she was sorry. "I admit to making fun of Hattie when she bawled most of the summer. Now I understand what she went through!"

Elmo sensed this was a women's discussion. Nodding to Mrs. Thomas, he called Trix and they left.

After Elmo was gone, Elma turned to Mrs. Thomas and repeated how sorry she was for her actions. "I'm not able to talk about it now, but when I get better control of myself, I will confide my problem to you."

Mrs. Thomas thought that certainly sounded like a mess in the making. Aloud, she agreed with Elma. "Yes, that will work better. I've had quite enough upsets for today." Elma thanked her and walked off toward the community building.

Mrs. Thomas realized that with all the goings-on, she had forgotten to ask Elmo to fix the squeaky screen door. She decided to walk over and ask him tomorrow after supper.

After settling that, she leisurely rocked the swing and pondered the day's events. Maybe she would have been better off if she hadn't opened a rooming house. She made extra trouble for herself—that was certain. On the other hand, if she had a calling to help others, didn't it stand to reason she needed to be in touch with people? And what better way than to have them living with you?

Elmo said the Bible was a guidepost, but Mrs. Thomas needed to become skilled in understanding it. She aimed to ask Elmo some questions when she saw him the next evening. She knew he had knowledge of the Bible, although she didn't know why she had that idea. He also had a tendency to change the subject when she talked about verses she was reading.

Tired of thinking about it, she decided to have some strawberries. It wasn't her habit to eat after supper, but she had an urge to do so now. There was no whipped cream left for the berries. *I wish that was the only problem I have to face. Goodness!*

When she finished, she snuggled in bed under her grandmother's quilt and fell to sleep feeling quite content.

Chapter 2

Mrs. Thomas breathed a sigh of relief when the girls did not dally over supper. She had waited all day to drop by Elmo's place and ask him if he would fix the squeaky screen door. As it turned out, there would be plenty of time to sit and talk if Elmo was so inclined.

As the town's handyman, he knew the goings-on in the area. And as a friend, he confided in her. She, of course, did not care to know other people's business; however, she did enjoy her frequent conversations with Elmo.

As Mrs. Thomas walked out the front door, she saw Hattie and Kate sitting in the swing and Mandy on the top step. She explained, "I am going to Elmo's to ask him to fix the screen door as the squeakin' about drives some people crazy." Hattie's face colored slightly, and she assumed a defensive position but offered no response. Mrs. Thomas waved and off she went before Hattie could start to cry.

Walking down the lane early in the evening was a special treat. The valley took on a whole new look in the dimming light of the evening sun. It presented itself as a sea of grass, changing color as it waved in the evening breeze. Occasionally, a bird sang a soft lullaby to quiet all nature. It worked. The atmosphere became a praise service to the Creator. Mrs. Thomas sauntered on, enjoying the sense of peace.

Nearing Elmo's place, she could see him sitting in the yard working on some machinery. He didn't notice her approaching in the shadow of the trees.

"Hey, Elmo! Can't you see you've got company?" As he heard Mrs. Thomas call, Elmo dropped his tools and grinned at her.

"You are one sneaky woman, Annie. Even old Trix is still asleep." He stood up to greet her and offered her a chair. What are you up to this fine evening?"

Old Trix eagerly jumped up to greet Mrs. Thomas. She rubbed his ears and sweet-talked to him, causing him to bounce with excitement. He loved the way she showed her affection for him. They had a special bond, those two.

"It looks like Trix will get all the attention tonight." Elmo sat down and looked to be pouting. "Annie, I declare I'm giving that dog to you. Talk about two peas in a pod!"

Mrs. Thomas laughed and took the chair Elmo offered. "I know it will snow on the fourth of July before that dog is mine."

"You are right about that, for sure. But back to my question— what are you doing rambling about this fine evening?"

"Well, I have a minor job I need done before some of my gals up and move."

He laughed. "Oh, this is serious. Maybe I should get at it now. We don't want you to lose your income, now do we? What's the job?"

"It's not that serious—it's the screen door. It has squeaked for several years, so a few more days can't matter. Frankly, I like the sound. It comforts me somehow."

"I know what you mean, Annie. It sounds like home and family for sure. There are many sounds from our childhood that bring comfort, and some that bring troubled thoughts, even when we are older. Is that the way it is?"

"You know, Elmo, it never ceases to amaze me how you can hone in on something and understand completely. I hate to bring this up, but I do want to thank you for looking after me yesterday evening. I went off the deep end. Here I thought I was strong all along, and I find I am as weak as any other. I'm glad Elma didn't confide in me. I doubt I could handle both her load and mine!"

"Annie, you expect too much of yourself. There are more problems in the world than any one person can handle. Besides, didn't the Savior in your attic Bible state He came to bear our burdens?"

"Elmo Martin, how did you know that? You must know more than you let on. I thought you said you didn't know much about the Bible."

"Well, I'll tell you this much. I do know more than I ever let on. I didn't mean to deceive you. It is just something I can't talk about now and maybe not ever."

Mrs. Thomas's curiosity was immediately aroused, but something inside warned her to keep silent and respect Elmo's position on the subject.

Silence fell over them and they sat in the quiet of the evening, both immersed in their thoughts. Old Trix lay as close to Annie's feet as he could get. She didn't appear to mind and kept her feet still. He loved her.

After a while, Mrs. Thomas stirred and old Trix jumped up. He knew his special time was over. "I best be on my way, Elmo. I thank you for a pleasant evening and for sharing Trix with me."

Hearing his name, Trix excitedly rubbed against Mrs. Thomas's legs. He wanted to jump up and kiss her face but knew that would raise Elmo's rough voice. So instead, he wiggled. Annie leaned over and kissed his face. In his best voice, he tried to tell her how much he loved her. She seemed to understand and bent down, whispering in his ear, "I love you too, old Trix."

"Annie, I've enjoyed this visit, but you'd best be getting on home before dark."

"Thank you for this pleasant evening, Elmo. Do you have an idea when you can get over?"

"I should be able to come over tomorrow, just about in time for supper." With that, he let out a big laugh.

Mrs. Thomas decided to call his bluff. "I have leftovers from supper tonight. I'd welcome some help in getting rid of them!"

"You are some gal, Annie. Your leftovers would suit me just fine. I'll be there with bells on, as they say."

Walking home, Mrs. Thomas wondered if the ladies would think it strange if Elmo came to supper. Most of them invited a gentleman to the Tuesday night visitor's supper from time to time. Elmo was a longtime friend, so no one should think twice about it.

She and Elmo had joked about his coming for supper as far back as she could remember. She couldn't think why he hadn't come, not even one time!

As she trekked on in the dusk, a lonely feeling swept over her. She felt sad but didn't know why. She almost wished she were back at Elmo's, talking or even sitting in comfortable silence.

Mrs. Thomas continued quickly up the lane in the rapidly cooling air. Arriving at her house, she found the girls sitting on the front porch. Hattie, Kate, and Mandy were in the swing, all pushing in unison to keep the back and forth motion steady. Elma sat on the top step with a book resting on her lap, but she was not reading it.

Mrs. Thomas pulled up a rocker and alighted on the thick stitched cushions. She was proud of the homey way her front porch looked.

Sitting there in the late rays of daylight, they were startled by the sudden approach of a man. Mrs. Thomas stood up and inquired if she could be of help to him. He looked and spoke like a gentleman.

"I would like to speak to Hattie for a short while, if I may. My name is Charlie Caldor from west of Bloomington. I am here for only a short time—otherwise, I would wait until tomorrow to talk to her."

Mrs. Thomas felt her jaw drop. She drew herself up and assumed her most dignified posture. "I think you might see Hattie in the parlor if she's agreeable to that, Mr. Caldor. What do you say to that, Hattie?"

Hattie, who could cry or faint at the drop of a hat, responded with quiet resolve. "I will speak with you for a short time in the parlor, Mr. Caldor, since Mrs. Thomas has granted us permission."

As Hattie and Mr. Caldor went to the parlor, everyone else traipsed into the kitchen. Mrs. Thomas sat on the rocker in the corner of the room and considered this surprising turn of events. *Who said there was nothing new under the sun?* Realizing this thought had come from the Bible, she continued her musing. *If everything that happens to us has happened to some poor soul before us, why should we worry? It just goes to show that if we live long enough, we will outlive our problems!* When Mrs. Thomas realized the fallacy of that remark, she threw her head back and laughed the way she'd seen Elmo do so many times.

The girls all gaped at Mrs. Thomas and wondered if she had finally lost it. She noticed their stares and started to cough, hoping to disguise her laugh. The ladies were so curious about what was happening in the parlor that their attention quickly returned there. Tension was high. Everyone had an opinion about what was going on. They tried to act calm and uninterested, but the façade didn't work.

Mrs. Thomas gazed at the girls. They were each reacting in their own way. Elma sat with a book in her hand, staring intently at it. She wasn't turning the pages and her eyes never moved across the page. Kate had a distressed look on her face as she wrung her hands and squirmed in her chair. Mandy had a look of distain on her face and casually looked about the room as if nothing unusual was happening.

Mrs. Thomas wondered about her own reaction. She had never heard the wall clock ticked so loudly. The flickering lamp created moving shadows on the ceiling. She began to wring her hands.

Chapter 3

Finally, Hattie and Charlie emerged from the parlor. All the kitchen sitters breathed a sigh of relief. Now they could find out what was going on! However, to their disappointment, Hattie charged up to her room without speaking a word.

Mrs. Thomas was stunned. How could Hattie leave them in such suspense? She didn't want to nose into her business, for goodness sake, but sometimes an explanation was needed— and this was one of those times!

Later that night, after the other ladies had gone to their rooms, Hattie tiptoed down the stairs and confided in Mrs. Thomas about what had happened. It turned out Charlie had a child—a daughter named Hannah. Hattie felt taking on someone else's daughter was a bit more than she could tackle. Charlie admitted he spoiled Hannah to make up for her not having a mother. He tried to assure Hattie they could work it out together.

Mrs. Thomas tossed and turned that night—her mind on Hattie, Charlie, and Hannah. The next day rolled around as all the others, yet nothing felt the same. Something was wrong. How could one situation change things so drastically?

The day slipped by quickly, and suddenly it was time for supper. To Mrs. Thomas's surprise, Elmo came driving up in his wagon. Would wonders never cease! They had kidded each other many times about his coming to supper—but this time he came!

Mrs. Thomas scurried to add another place at the table. She always cooked plenty, so she had no worries of running low on food. The supper was tasty, and Elmo kept them entertained and laughing.

Charlie stopped by to pick up Hattie so she could go with him to meet Hannah and start getting acquainted with her. Hattie looked as if she might not go but then surprised everyone by bracing herself and marching off.

After Hattie left, Elmo said he had a surprise for them, but he would not reveal it until the kitchen and dining room were spotless. Eager to learn about the surprise, Mrs. Thomas and the ladies jumped up to do the dinner cleanup. They carried the dishes into the kitchen and wrapped goodies to send home with Elmo.

Mrs. Thomas inspected the dining room to be sure all was in order. As she turned to leave the room, the heel of her shoe caught on the carpet, and she went flying to the floor. She tried to catch herself with her hand, causing her to twist her wrist when she landed. She cried out in pain.

Elmo rushed in and helped her to the parlor, where he eased her onto the settee. Examining her swelling wrist, he determined it was severely sprained. He asked if someone would get some pain medicine.

While Kate hurried to get the medicine, Elmo went to his wagon and brought back some ice, which he wrapped in a towel and place on Mrs. Thomas's wrist. Kate returned with the pain medicine and helped her take it. Joining Mrs. Thomas on the settee, Elmo propped her arm on a pillow.

Kate and Mandy went to the kitchen to finish cleaning up, and Elma double-checked the dining room.

Mrs. Thomas felt embarrassed about falling and tried to explain her feelings to Elmo. "I never fall. I hurried—that's all. I deserved to fall for acting so foolish."

"You know you aren't the first one to fall, Annie, nor the last. Now what do you think of those words of wisdom?"

Smiling, she shook her head. She did not want to speak for fear her voice would betray the severity of her wrist pain. Her large blue eyes studied Elmo as he continued.

"You know, I learned to feel for sprains and such by workin' with the farm animals all these years. Does that worry you?"

"It's a comfort to know you weren't practicin' on me," Mrs. Thomas managed to answer. "Seriously, I thank you for fixin' me up."

Mrs. Thomas felt she should update Elmo on what was happening with Hattie. She briefly explained the situation and told him that Charlie had taken Hattie to meet his Hannah, and they would return later.

"I did wonder about it. Thanks for filling me in, Annie. Life is funny, for sure. It seems to be fine, and then all at once it unravels. There are a few things I have never been able understand."

Mrs. Thomas wondered what in the world was he referring to. It must be something that had happened before she opened her rooming house in this area. Was there no end of things she had to worry about? Turning to more positive thoughts, she mused, *Hmmm. Someday I'll have to tell the ladies all about how Elmo and I met. That would make a fine porch swing tale.*

Chapter 4

The girls made fast time getting the kitchen work done. They didn't seem to mind Elmo's bossiness—telling them no surprise until the supper dishes were done. He stayed in the sitting room and visited with Mrs. Thomas while the girls finished their work.

Mrs. Thomas asked Elmo how it happened that he decided to visit this evening. He shrugged his shoulders, got up, and walked to the door. He then turned to face her but didn't say anything right away. She noticed the girls talking in the kitchen and heard the rattle of dishes while she waited for his reply.

"You know, I've lived alone for a long time and never minded at all. My old Trix keeps me good company. He understands me and I understand him. Now you may think that is odd— and maybe it is—but that dog is family to me."

"Don't worry about it, Elmo. There are odd areas in my life, as well. Except I don't feel they are odd. I feel they are all natural."

"That's just how I think about it, Anna. You know, after you left last evening, somehow the place seemed empty. I can't explain it—we didn't even talk that much. But when you left, I suddenly felt lonesome." He broke out laughing. "I thought, 'Shoot, I got an invite to that gal's house, so why don't I use it?' And here I am!"

"Well, for heaven's sake, Elmo. I have known you all these years and never have I heard you talk so much. And since when have you needed an invite to my place?"

The women tumbled out of the kitchen and, pulling off their aprons, headed to the porch. On the way, Elma peeked in the sitting room and laughingly remarked, "Hey, Elmo! That screen door still squeaks!"

Elmo chuckled. "Hey, gal, don't betray my secret. That squeak is my meal ticket!"

With a mischievous grin, Elma replied, "Why don't you just rent a room? Then you'll get supper every night." With a toss of her head, she slipped out the door.

Mrs. Thomas and Elmo looked at each other and grinned, acknowledging that Elma had won that round.

"Anna, let's go outside and I will show you my surprise." Elmo helped Mrs. Thomas get up—although she felt quite capable of getting up herself—and they headed for the porch. Mandy Jayne jumped up and offered her place on the swing to Mrs. Thomas.

Mrs. Thomas looked around. The evening was most pleasant with a faint breeze. The leaves waving in the breeze looked like dancers frolicking individually, yet in perfect harmony.

"Anna, didn't you hear me? Or are you ignoring me?" Elmo's voice broke into her thoughts.

"Yes, I heard you ask to have supper with us every night." *Hmm. I shouldn't have said that—but he didn't seem to notice.*

"I asked you what flavor ice cream you wanted." He pulled large pieces of burlap back, revealing an ice-cream freezer—no, there were two freezers! Well, what about that! He was a man full of surprises.

The girls were overjoyed to see the treat. Elma scurried into the kitchen to get bowls and spoons. As Elmo removed the freezer lids, Mrs. Thomas's eyes lit up at the delicious looking ice cream. Chocolate and vanilla both looking creamy, smooth, and firm. "Is there anything better than a dish of homemade ice cream on a beautiful evening?"

Kate took Mrs. Thomas a bowl with both flavors in it. "Elmo said since you didn't say what flavor you wanted, he gave you a dip of both."

Hattie placed a small table by the swing within easy reach of Mrs. Thomas's good hand.

"This is a perfect treat, Elmo. I know you made it—goodness, who knew you had so many talents?"

"I didn't want the ice I worked hard for last winter to go to waste. My neighbor Hank goes to the river and helps me cut the ice into blocks and haul them home to the icehouse. We lay a row of ice the length of the icehouse and cover it with sawdust. We lay one row of ice blocks on top of the other, until the icehouse is full to the top. It keeps frozen all summer long and makes a lot of ladies happy on warm summer evenings."

Mrs. Thomas looked at Elmo, thinking he sure was getting gabby. "You are right about that. I can't think of a better evening—wrist sprain and all." All the ladies laughed and nodded their agreement as they continued to enjoy their treat.

The girls began to get in the spirit of things. Kate declared she would not mind enjoying a similar treat every few days. As the laughter started, Mrs. Thomas noticed someone approaching. As they drew near, she saw Hattie with Charlie and Hannah.

"Well, look who's here. You planned it well—just in time for ice cream. It is Elmo's surprise for us. Sit here in the swing by me, Hattie."

Hattie introduced Hannah to the ladies before she sat down. "Ladies, I'd like you to meet Charlie's daughter, Hannah." As they started to tell Hannah their names, she looked at her father in a most unhappy manner.

"Daddy, may we leave now?"

Charlie was uncomfortable and showed it. With a red face, he tried to smooth things over. "Come, Hannah. I can't wait to try some ice cream. Let's sit here on the swing while we eat."

The crisis passed as they sat down. However, Hannah sat on her father's knee—the one that separated Hattie from Charlie. Hattie turned pink, and Charlie looked highly displeased.

"Oh, my," thought Mrs. Thomas. She saw trouble brewing. She wondered, *Why does there always seem to be a fly in the ointment? Why can't things go right for once? It seems as though I've traveled this road before.*

Giving herself a shake, she returned to the present and heard Elmo trying to cover the embarrassment by drawing Charlie into a conversation. "How are things in your part of the country, Charlie?"

"We sure could use some rain about . . ."

Hannah prevented Charlie from further speech by handing him her ice cream. "Daddy, this ice cream isn't as good as our ice cream, and I don't want it."

Charlie started to respond but Hannah interrupted him. "Let's go home, just you and me. OK?"

Hattie's face turned red, and Mrs. Thomas could tell she was on the verge of tears. Not that she blamed her. The tension was breaking up a good time. She must do something—but not interfere, of course. "I wouldn't worry about it too much. Children often get their nose put of joint when someone new comes on the scene, if you get my drift."

No one responded. The girls scurried around picking up ice-cream bowls to wash and put away. Elmo covered the ice cream with the burlap. All tried to cover their embarrassment.

Elmo gave a "thanks and good-bye" and headed for home and old Trix.

Hattie and Charlie remained in the swing with Hannah on her father's knee. All three seemed frozen to the spot—as if they shared a space in Elmo's icehouse. Hannah glared at Charlie.

Mrs. Thomas felt at a loss for words for the first time in her life. She had to do something quickly. "Look, Charlie, you come back and visit again. I have visitors' night for supper on Tuesdays, if you can make it."

Charlie and Hattie looked uncomfortable. Hannah pulled her father's hand and asked him to take her home.

"Thank you for the invitation, Mrs. Thomas." Charlie turned and whispered a few words to Hattie. Then he walked off, Hannah skipping at his side with a big smile on her face.

Head hanging, Hattie retreated into the house. Mrs. Thomas thought if she were keeping a scorecard, Hannah would have won the first round.

If she had said it one time, she had said it a dozen. "Life deals us a good hand, and fate snatches it away." She moved her sprained wrist to a better position and then voiced her thoughts. "Hattie is in for a rough time, sure as shootin'."

The ladies made quick work of gathering the rest of the ice-cream dishes and then disappeared into the house. Mrs. Thomas sat quietly in the swing, rhythmically moving it back and forth. She could not get Hattie off her mind. She wanted to think of a way to help her, if possible. "It needs to be done carefully, as I don't want to give the appearance of meddling," she murmured to herself. "I always make it a rule not to nose in other people's business." She had a calling, and she expected to help and to give advice. She did not call that being a busybody!

Mrs. Thomas recalled a poem she had written a few years earlier. A mother hummingbird wanted her son to help others. Nevertheless, when son hummingbird gave a ride to friend bumblebee, Mrs. Hummingbird sang, "Do all you can to help others, but don't come home with pollen on your feathers."

Mrs. Hummingbird wanted to instill good qualities in her son, yet she hindered his mission. Mrs. Thomas thought about it. *Do I try to justify myself? Do I meddle? Do I hinder my calling by wondering if I meddle?*

Hattie came out the screen door and saved Mrs. Thomas from further agonizing by joining her on the swing. Mrs. Thomas looked at Hattie's face. She thought, *If I never see that look on a face again, it would be too soon.*

Hattie pulled a hankie from her pocket and covered her face with it. Then the tears flowed—she wept without reserve. When her hanky was drenched, Mrs. Thomas offered her own handkerchief.

"Mrs. Thomas, I hardly know where to start. I need to talk to someone in the worst way. I don't have the right to impose on you. It's just that . . ."

"Hold on there, Hattie. If you need help, then you need help. There's no use in sputtering about it. I am not one, as you know, to involve myself in others' affairs. However, it appears you need help, and you need it now. Why don't you start at the beginning and tell me what's in your heart."

Hattie haltered as she began her story. Mrs. Thomas thought, *I wouldn't place a dime on her finishing it—if I were a gambler, that is.*

After soaking several hankies, Hattie grabbed Mrs. Thomas's hand and began. Mrs. Thomas thought the front porch swing was an excellent place for Hattie to pour out her heart.

"Most of my life, I felt left out and missed out on most of the good things my brothers and sisters experienced. I was the oldest child, and my parents expected more of me. At least, that's how I felt—I am not so sure of that now. We don't see ourselves as others see us. I know that for a fact."

Mrs. Thomas thought of all the "what people didn't know" things in her own life. "Go on, Hattie, and tell me how you feel. I'll be here for as long as you need me."

Mrs. Thomas's mind strayed back to a time she had sat alongside the bed of another broken heart. Aw, that hurt yet when her mind recalled it. *Lela, poor Lela. She had a load to carry. She and Derek were so much in love, but she couldn't make herself tell Derek she cared about him. Lela had been raised to believe that nice girls don't reveal personal feelings to boys.*

The fact that Lela had been married and divorced and was the mother of two little girls overwhelmed her. She was afraid to tell Derek for fear he wouldn't want her. She started to once but lost her nerve.

Then one fateful day, Derek took Lela to the park, where he introduced his mother to her. They were enjoying the conversation and the dishes of ice cream when Lela's world was tumbled by the next event.

Wouldn't you know, that very day Lela's aunt chose to take the girls for a surprise visit to see Lela. It was a surprise all right, especially when the girls ran up and threw themselves on Lela, screaming "Mama!" Derek couldn't accept that she hadn't trusted him enough to confide her situation to him. Lela couldn't bring herself to tell him how she loved him and that she was petrified of losing him. Others had shunned her because of her divorce. What would she do if Derek reacted like those other people? Could she chance losing him?

Suddenly, Mrs. Thomas came back to the present. She was glad to leave those sad memories. Hattie drew a deep breath and heaved a sigh. Then with her lips quivering and her eyes glistening with tears, she began to take Mrs. Thomas on a journey to her world.

Mrs. Thomas felt since this was her calling, she needed to get out of the past and listen to Hattie.

Chapter 5

Hattie shifted her position a bit and turned to face Mrs. Thomas. "Well, as I said, all my life I felt uncomfortable and different. I never fit in with the crowd and always worried what others thought of me."

Mrs. Thomas pulled another handkerchief from her pocket, noting as she did it was one of her favorites. What could she do? To run and get another now would interrupt Hattie's story, and they might not get into it again. She sighed and turned the hanky over to Hattie.

"This seems silly to you, I'm sure—and I feel silly saying it—but I am touchy and I do hurt easily. The boys used to gather around and tease me until I cried. To their delight, I never failed to cry."

She rose from the swing and walked to and fro, shoulders slumped as if the confession was too heavy for her. "Over the years, I have tried to overcome my self-doubts—without success. To make a long story short, I met Charlie. He treats me with respect and makes me feel as though I am indeed someone special. The years I doubted my worth have vanished. He fills me with self-confidence."

Mrs. Thomas was ready to offer a reply when Hattie, whose face glowed with thoughts of Charlie, suddenly dropped her head and in utter despair wailed, "That is until his daughter came on the scene!"

Mrs. Thomas stood and gathered Hattie in her arms. She felt at a total loss for words. She often thought of comforting words she would say to people if the opportunity ever arose. Now her mind was akin to the blocks of ice in Elmo's icehouse. Frozen!

Both returned to the swing and pushed it slowly back and forth. Knowing Hattie expected words of great wisdom from her, Mrs. Thomas took her hand and gave it a gentle squeeze. She feared she could not live up to her calling!

They sat there for a long spell sharing the solitude of the evening. Hattie was the first to break the silence.

"I know why I see you swinging here so often, alone even. It is soothing for some reason. And I feel better after talking to you."

Mrs. Thomas knew Hattie had only just begun her battle. An unknown force released her tongue, and she felt words coming to her mind. Possibly, she could help Hattie after all. "As I see it, there is a big problem. It must be identified and then faced. I think you will agree we must first find the cause, and after that we can figure out how to fix it."

Hattie looked as if she had just been handed an impossible task. "That sounds so confusing. I wouldn't know where to start; I am not a problem solver." Hattie began to wring her hands, and it was obvious another tear-time was close.

The thought of her last favorite hanky, safe in her apron pocket, fluttered briefly in Mrs. Thomas's mind. She wondered what made her think she could help anyone. What could she do? She decided to offer up a prayer, even though she had not prayed this way for some time. It couldn't hurt. Silently, she prayed a short, but sincere, plea for help.

"All right, Hattie, if you had to name the first problem here, what would you say?"

She was sure of the problem and wasn't long in expressing it. "Hannah doesn't like me. Her feelings will end my relationship with Charlie, I fear."

Mrs. Thomas felt that was certainly a strong possibility. Since Hattie had touched on the subject, Mrs. Thomas followed. "OK, that's a start. Can you think of any reasons for her dislike?"

Hattie's facial expression suggested she was giving the matter serious thought. "I don't know why she wouldn't like me. We've only just met. I suppose she might not want to share her father. However, most likely I'm being too sensitive. I admitted to that earlier."

Mrs. Thomas felt good that she had helped Hattie get a handle on the issue. She thought maybe she was better than she knew. Immediately, she was ashamed and knew she should not have those prideful feelings. Afraid she would fall flat on her face with such vain thoughts, she admitted she had done nothing except to get Hattie to think and figure it out for herself.

"It looks as if you have a good handle on the situation, Hattie. What course of action will you take?"

"I need help with that. I'm short on ideas. What would you do?" Hattie got up, left the porch, and began pacing in the grass.

Mrs. Thomas wanted to pace in the grass as well. What could Hattie do? Somehow, Hattie had to gain Hannah's confidence. How could she get the child to accept her? *Well, so much for my calling.* Then it dawned on her. Hannah felt left out the same as Hattie did!

She jumped up from the swing and joined Hattie as she walked in the grass.

"Now, as I see it, Hannah is afraid of losing her father. She may be small, but she is aware there is something special between you and Charlie. She also has been the center of attention since her mother has been gone. You are a threat to her. I would assume there has been spoiling going on as well. Charlie may be trying to make up to her for the loss of her mother."

Hattie stopped pacing and turned to face Mrs. Thomas. "I think you are right. Where did get all your wisdom?"

"Goodness, Hattie, I don't have any great wisdom. I will admit I whispered a prayer before we got started. So what do you think about that?"

Hattie looked slightly embarrassed but admitted she had been raised in a praying home. However, she had drifted away from God—why or when, she didn't remember.

Mrs. Thomas sat down on the swing and beckoned Hattie to sit beside her. When she settled, Mrs. Thomas took her hand. "I may be bold, but I wonder if we could say a prayer together. I believe you will find help for this matter."

They bowed their heads and joined hands. Softly they began to make their needs known to the One they believed could help them. Tears rolled down their cheeks as they realized their negligence and felt the sorrow of wasted time.

As their tears freely flowed, both experienced deep sorrow in their heart. However, a sweet peace and a release from fear overcame them. Their hearts told them they had done the right thing.

Hattie spoke first, proclaiming she had never experienced such feelings. However, she felt there was more she needed to do. Mrs. Thomas agreed. She had experienced some of this in younger years. "We need to follow through to learn and search what His will is for us."

"Thank you, Mrs. Thomas. You helped me more than I thought possible. My plan of action is to center my attention on Hannah. It will be Hannah and me, with Charlie as the extra one." She laughed and remarked, "'Course, Charlie might not like that!"

Mrs. Thomas laughed with Hattie. "This is only the start, you know. The battle is just beginning. Love and patience are tools you will need, and I'm here to give you a hand when needed."

The screen door squeaked and they turned their heads to see Elma walking out the door. "You two look up to something, for sure." They looked at each other, not knowing how to respond. Elma continued, "I don't see a cat—however, I'm sure one got your tongues."

Mrs. Thomas shook her head and stuck out her tongue. Hattie followed her example, laughingly sticking out her tongue as well. Just then, Kate and Mandy rounded the corner from the backyard where they had been inspecting their flower garden. Coming upon Mrs. Thomas and Hattie with their tongues sticking out, Kate's and Mandy's mouths dropped open.

"Kate, do you see what I see, or am I imagining it?" Mandy Jayne shook her head. "We'd better leave—it might be catching!"

Kate laughed and said she felt they must be seeing things.

"Maybe we should go back to the garden. What do you think?"

"It's all Elma's fault," Mrs. Thomas declared. At that statement, Elma stuck out her tongue, and everyone roared with laughter.

Suddenly, Hattie stiffened and looked stricken. Mrs. Thomas looked to see what had startled her. There stood Charlie! *Oh, just what we need. Now what?*

"If I didn't know better, I would say I have come upon ladies with their tongues sticking out. Now, I'm not qualified as a judge but I have never seen such a sight in my life."

The girls all jumped in to explain what had happened. Chuckling, Charlie held up his hand and asked if he could speak to Hattie. She walked toward him, trying to act normal. She looked back at Mrs. Thomas, who gave her a slight nod and held her hands in a prayerful position. Hattie smiled and walked off with Charlie.

Hattie returned later with a different look to her face. Mrs. Thomas figured she must have shared her plans about Hannah with Charlie.

Out of all the days in her life, Mrs. Thomas had never experienced one such as this. And she was tired to the bone! She eagerly crawled into her feather bed and welcomed the comfort it provided.

Before drifting off to sleep, she heard sobbing coming from Elma's room. She thought she should see about her, but since Elma didn't care to discuss things, Mrs. Thomas felt her hands were tied. With these thoughts still rumbling around in her head, she drifted off into the quiet land of sleep.

Chapter 6

The next morning Mrs. Thomas was eager to finish breakfast and head for the mill to pick up her baking needs for the weekend. She figured as long as she was over that way, she might as well drop by Mrs. Lang's and see how she was faring. Kate had mentioned Mrs. Lang's oldest girl had told her about some disturbing family matters.

She had a perfect right to check into the matter if there was trouble. Hadn't she helped Hattie with her trouble? Remembering that brought a feeling of discomfort to Mrs. Thomas. This morning Hattie had declined breakfast. Granted, she didn't ever eat much. However, she had never before failed to have breakfast with us.

Hattie remarked she faced a busy day. Some unfinished business, she said, and away she went, toting a large satchel. Hattie was the town's only tailor. Her work was in demand by most of the town's women. At times, when a client was in a hurry for a tailoring need, she brought the work home. Perhaps she was carrying clients' clothing in the satchel.

Mrs. Thomas noticed the satchel was bulging. In fact, Hattie was struggling with the weight of it. Mrs. Thomas could not avoid wondering, *What in the world does she have in it? That looks too heavy to be clients' clothing.* Since she wasn't one to meddle in other's affairs, she didn't say anything. However, she did wonder.

Mrs. Thomas set out for the Lang's house. There wasn't a soul in sight. Sighing, she turned and made her way to the mill, thinking nothing newsworthy would happen that day.

After Mrs. Thomas made her purchases and exchanged a few words with the mill workers, she made her way home. The load she carried was lighter than the load on her mind.

The sound of the old Monan broke into her thoughts. She put her supplies down and waited for it to run past. The Monon roared down the tracks, blowing her mournful call. All at once, Mrs. Thomas felt great—she was a kid once more.

The train faded from view and so did the elation she felt. As she ambled on, thinking of the day's duties, she was stopped short by some yelling and a loud commotion. "Mrs. Thomas, Mrs. Thomas! Wait for me! I need you to help me!"

Turning around, she saw Mrs. Lang heading her way as fast as the old Monon and almost as noisy. "My lands, slow down, Mrs. Lang, before you break a leg."

"But you don't understand. I did something I've never done before. My ma told me you could only push a man so far. Well, I think I did it!"

"Calm down. Come sit on this log with me and tell me what in the world is wrong." *Goodness. And I had thought this would be an eventless day.* "Whatever did you do that was so wrong?"

Mrs. Lang hesitated, breathing long and deep. "I have done many things before. I know you remember when I took all James' clothes while he slept, and he had to leave wearing only his long johns and a blanket."

Mrs. Thomas also remembered when he returned the next day to pick up his clothes. Mrs. Lang had chased him around the yard with her broom. She was a slight woman—not a bit of fat on her bones—but oh, so strong. 'Course, he had run off! She remembered well. She tried to hide a smile by covering it with a cough. Mrs. Lang was too engrossed in her problems to notice.

"You may be aware my husband has returned. I do not want him around. He doesn't have a place to sleep at home because I turned our bedroom into a room for my girls, and they love it!"

"That doesn't seem to be such a big problem. Does he know about the new arrangement?" To Mrs. Thomas, the problem was not as bad as she had feared.

"Oh, that's not all. Here's the problem. When the girls and I moved the bed, one leg caught on a floorboard. It flew up, revealing what was under it. Do you know what it was?"

"No, I have not an inkling, Mrs. Lang. What did you discover?" Well, she admitted it—she was hoping to find out what was going on at the Lang's. It looked as though she had hit pay dirt!

Immediately, Mrs. Thomas felt shame for equating poor Mrs. Lang's problems to hitting pay dirt. There were times when she felt she should have been a rabbit dog rather than the mistress of a rooming house. Both she and the rabbit dog were always sniffing things out. Sighing deeply, she studied Mrs. Lang's face. *She would be so pretty if she didn't have such a worn look.* She turned her attention back to Mrs. Lang's story.

"I could not believe it. Under the board were wads of money! Nine hundred dollars! Now where do you suppose he got all that money? He could have used it to support us. I sent the older girls out to work while all that money was hidden under the bed I slept in!"

Mrs. Thomas was surprised. "All right, I understand why you got angry. But what did you do that was so bad, if I may ask?" She thought there weren't enough bad things Mrs. Lang could do to him. He deserved whatever he got!

In a quivering voice, Mrs. Lang continued. "Yesterday, he came back yelling, 'This is my house, and you can't turn me out!' Then he raved when he saw the girls had the bedroom. He must have remembered the money about then because he forced the girls from the room and slammed the door shut. We heard grunts and groans and huffing and puffing and the sounds of furniture scraping the floor."

Mrs. Thomas exclaimed, "Oh, dear!" and held her breath for fear of what happened when Mr. Lang discovered the money wasn't there.

"When he discovered the money was gone, we heard sounds like wood breaking and the screams of a wild animal. It was a moment I will never forget—the memory gives me chills even now. The girls and I fled the house and hid out until this morning."

Mrs. Lang continued her tale of woe. "When I sneaked back into the house, I couldn't believe my eyes. He had a pallet of blankets on the floor and had rolled up in one. He was snoring so loudly, it's a wonder he didn't wake himself up."

Mrs. Lang hung her head and stopped talking. Mrs. Thomas felt this was going to be a wasted day after all. She didn't know much more than she had at the first. Plus, she was on her last nerve!

Then Mrs. Lang blurted out what happened in one breath and didn't stop until she finished. "As soon as I was sure he was asleep, I rushed into the kitchen where I had two large tubs of water ready to do the wash this morning. I filled a large bucket with water and poured it all over him. While he was struggling to get untangled from the blanket, I poured another full bucket of water over him. I made my way out of the house in a hurry, and then I saw you."

"My, my, will wonders never cease? Where are the children?" Mrs. Thomas questioned.

In a trembling voice, Mrs. Lang said she had sent them off earlier with a filled picnic basket and told them to go and enjoy the day. They had gone to a play hut in the woods for a "fun day."

No sooner had Mrs. Lang finished describing her problem than they heard the roar of her angry husband. He ran toward them, another spectacle in the making, his thin, wiry body wrapped in a sopping wet blanket. Mrs. Thomas never imagined she would see that sight again, but there he was. Clearly, trouble was ahead. She had no idea what to expect. If he tried to harm his wife, could she stop him?

She heard a loud familiar voice a ways behind her. Turning, she saw Elmo! She could hardly believe her eyes. Even old Trix was with him.

By the time Mr. Lang reached his wife, he had worked one arm out of his cocoon. He raised his voice and his arm to threaten his wife.

Without warning, Trix, who was near enough to hear and see the threat, ran toward the offender. He jumped up and grabbed for Mr. Lang's arm. Mr. Lang jerked his arm back, causing Trix to catch the blanket instead. He pulled and tugged and the blanket came off. There stood Mr. Lang in his long johns—again!

Elmo reached the group and called off Trix, who was enjoying his part in all this. Elmo told him to "sit" and he did. However, he continued to emit a low-throated growl.

"May I ask what in the world is going on here, Anna? I came around to help you bring home your baking supplies. I never expected to run into something like this!"

By this time, Mr. Lang had gotten over his scare from Trix. Walking up to Elmo and glaring at him with piercing blue eyes, he declared in a belligerent tone, "This matter is between my wife and me. I am leaving and taking my wife with me, and you had better keep that dog of yours away from me."

Mr. Lang had no idea who he was talking to. Elmo was not a man to mess with, especially when he sensed an injustice—and this was one, for sure.

Trix was still obeying his master's "sit" command but continued to growl. Elmo told Mr. Lang, "You had better stay where you are while I try to get at the truth."

"Watch him, Trix." Without a sound, old Trix jumped up and glared at Mr. Lang.

Elmo listened to the story as both Mrs. Thomas and Mrs. Lang tried to fill him in on the happenings. After they finished, Elmo told Mr. Lang to go with him to the constable's office. He advised Mrs. Lang to go home and see to her girls.

"Anna, I 'spect you best run along home. It's about lunchtime for your gals, isn't it? I might even drop in if I get this business taken care of in time."

Mrs. Lang laughed nervously. "I will go home now and see how the children are doing. I sure did make myself a big mess, didn't I? The floor is flooded with two big buckets of water! Thanks for your kindness and your help, Mrs. Thomas." Looking at Elmo, she acknowledged him. "Thanks to you too, sir."

As Mrs. Thomas walked home, she thought about the morning events. How could it all have happened in a few hours? Mrs. Lang sure had a story to tell. *My word, how would it feel to sleep above nine hundred dollars?* She also wondered how Mr. Lang came by all that money!

Something else bothered Mrs. Thomas. She wondered what Mrs. Lang had done with the nine hundred dollars. *Why, I should have asked her. I don't consider it prying. After all, she did involve me in this.*

She couldn't get her mind off the question of where the money was. Arriving home, she decided to read her attic Bible before fixing lunch—she had to get the foolish subject of that money off her mind.

She needed to get more instructions from her attic Bible. She did believe every word in it—and it gave her comfort. She guessed part of her problem might be that she couldn't understand why God, who had many to choose from, would want her.

She read how God loved the people He created. She meditated on the fact she was nothing but dust. And God sent His son, Jesus, to die for her. Yet she hadn't even thought of Him for years. Then she had found her attic Bible. She wondered if she would have continued on the same path of neglect if she hadn't found that Bible.

Well, enough of the woolgathering. There are four ladies coming home soon and hungry as lumberjacks. Time to set the table and get the food ready! With most of the morning already spent, she only had time to prepare a light lunch. Well, she would make an extra special supper to make up for it.

Mrs. Thomas's mind turned to Elmo and how he seemed to know a lot about the Bible—but said he didn't know much about it. *I really feel close to Elmo. We have clicked from the start. Hmmm . . . The start . . .*

ॐ

Mrs. Thomas remembered it well. It was when she was moving here. She was traveling on the bottom road, which tended to be muddy after a rain. As luck would have it, it had rained the day before she moved. The fellow she hired to move her thought they shouldn't take the bottom road, but Mrs. Thomas was persistent because it was the shortest route, and she was tired.

She wasn't familiar with the area or how hazardous the road was, but she found out soon enough. The wagon wheels sank in the mud and the horses lunged and lunged, exerting all their strength to pull the wagon out of the mud trap. The horses made one last surge. The wagon jerked and partially broke free, but in the process, it tipped over! Mrs. Thomas couldn't believe her eyes. There, for the entire world to see, were all her possessions soaking in the mud. The driver pulled out her few pieces of furniture and wiped the mud from them. He was at a loss as to what to do next, for articles of her clothing were strewn about and he was hesitant to pick them up. What would he do with them if he did pick them up?

Mrs. Thomas was reduced to tears. She would have to wade in the mud and retrieve her clothing. She would never wear her shoes again, and most likely, the mud would go over her shoe tops. Deciding there was no alternative, she headed into the mire.

Closing her eyes, she took a step into the mud. Then came a voice yelling and a dog barking. She stopped in her tracks and turned around. Losing her balance, she nearly fell in the muck. As she tried to regain her balance, an unknown object hit her leg and down she went into the thick of the mud!

Oh, what a day that was. Sitting in the mud, screaming her head off, she heard a loud deep voice yelling, "Trix, come here!" And some dog was barking its head off. When she opened her eyes, she saw a burly man and a despicable yapping dog. She also saw her driver trying to calm the horses, which were whinnying and jumping around. Mrs. Thomas had to laugh as she recalled it, although she had been fuming with anger that day.

After helping her out of the mud, Elmo had told her to grab some clothes that escaped the mud and follow him. He led her to the back of a barn and pointed to a long tub. "That's the horses' watering trough. Now when I leave, you get into that water and wash off the mud. Then put on your clean clothes. Leave the dirty clothes on the ground, and I'll pick them up later."

While Mrs. Thomas washed off the mud, Elmo went back to the wagon. He gathered all her clothes and put them in a large net. He then hung the net on a tree branch and lowered it into the stream, allowing the clear flowing water to wash away the mud.

Mrs. Thomas later hung her clothes on a line. They were perfectly clean and smelled so good after they dried. She didn't know it then, but that was the way Elmo always washed his clothes. He would soak them in soapy water all night. Then the next day, he put them in the net and let the stream of clean water rinse them!

Daydreaming over. It was time to call the girls for lunch.

Chapter 7

Supper was over and the ladies gathered on the front porch. Mrs. Thomas sat in her favorite spot on the swing—the left side. She had no idea why she favored this spot, but she did. Mandy and Kate shared the swing with her. Elma sat on the top step—her favorite spot.

Elmo had stopped by earlier but couldn't stay for supper. He had dropped Mr. Lang off at the constable's office and left after explaining the events that had taken place. He didn't know what had happened to Mr. Lang since then.

The evening was perfect. All the earth was at peace, but peace did not prevail on the porch. Mrs. Thomas was distressed. If there was one place she wanted to be at peace, it was on the front porch in the swing.

As it was, no one was saying anything. Hattie had not come home from work that evening. No one knew what to say or do. Elma looked at the ground, pretending to be fascinated with some object there. Kate sniffed occasionally and wiped her eyes. Mandy, less timid than the others, broke the strained silence. "They say it's the silent ones who must be watched." A haughty toss of her head stressed her point.

Kate looked pained. Her gentle brown eyes glistened with tears. "We don't know what the facts are, Mandy, and we need to be careful what we say. Kate then became a "Mrs. Thomas" and began relating a story.

"I knew a young girl who was accused of stealing money from a classmate. Her nightmare began when she was walking home from school. Someone loudly asked her what she had done with the money. She had no idea what the girl was talking about and asked in innocence, 'What money?' Her accuser responded, 'The money you stole from the lunch box.' The girl was stunned with pain and embarrassment. In fact, she stopped going to school after that. She was humiliated to think she had been accused of stealing."

Mandy interjected her own thoughts. "How can you be sure that she didn't steal the money?"

Kate, although stressed, forged ahead. "That's a good question, Mandy. The way I saw it, if her guilt couldn't be proved or disproved, how could they accuse her? They had no way of knowing the truth."

Mandy wasn't satisfied. "The accuser—did she have strong evidence?" She faced Kate eye-to-eye.

Kate paled at the question. "She thought she did. She said she saw the girl acting funny in the sewing room and noticed she was close to the lunch box where the money had been. The girl acted flustered and asked a question—something about not knowing how to use the iron. They thought she used the iron as an excuse for being nervous. Anyway, later when the owner of the lunch box went to get her money, it was no longer there."

Elma, who had been listening in silence, decided to add her opinion to the mix. "As I see it, I can understand how the nervous girl was thought to be guilty. I believe it myself."

"But she wasn't! I knew her, and I know she would never steal!" Kate was on the edge. Mrs. Thomas felt it was time to get to the real problem.

"I would be careful about judging anyone. I have spent time lately reading a Bible I found in the attic. You've seen me. I felt the need to get more spiritual in my life, and I have been reading the Bible every spare minute. It is a road map for people who are afraid or think there must be more to life than they have. What little I've read, I have tried to follow. The Bible says God is the judge. I don't know much about such things, but I aim to be careful about the way I judge people."

Without warning, Mrs. Thomas then brought up the subject in everyone's mind—the topic causing all the tension in the air. "Do any of you ladies have an idea where our absent boarder is?" The girls jumped in unison—one would think all had the same malady.

"Do you all know and are not telling me? Shouldn't I know what happened to Hattie? Mandy, you mentioned having to watch out for the silent ones. Now tell me, what did you mean by that?"

The ladies responded in various ways. Kate fiddled with her hands, deciding her nails needed attention. Elma jumped up from the step and busied herself looking for something in the grass. Mandy, the bold one, sat in the swing looking downcast. Then suddenly she spewed out things the rest had never heard her say.

"Enough is enough. Why should we sit around and try to act normal and pretend we don't know anything about Hattie? Every one of us knows exactly where Hattie is and why she left."

Hearing the gasps that followed her outburst, Mandy paused. Regaining her composure, she continued with new fervor. "She always acted as though she were a tad better than the rest of us. Her and her offended airs. Oh, we had her number, didn't we, girls? She acted like goody two-shoes around you, Mrs. Thomas, playing on your sympathy. She should go on the stage!"

Mrs. Thomas made no comment. Her heart was breaking. No matter what Hattie had done, she continued to believe she had been truthful when she told Mrs. Thomas how she had felt all her life. "Where is Hattie? What has she done?"

Mandy hung her head and looked sorry she had blurted everything out.

Kate voiced her thoughts. "I'm sorry all this happened. We have been on needles and pins, fearing something would happen, and now here we are."

Mrs. Thomas felt she would scream if someone didn't tell her what was going on.

Elma decided it was time for the truth to come out, and it looked as though she had to speak it. "Hattie has gone off with Charlie. That's why he came back to talk with her. I said I would be more afraid of Charlie than I would be of that snake. Rumor has it they are in Bloomington, where he has a house on Walnut Street. We saw her upstairs before breakfast this morning. She was rushing out of her room with her stuffed satchel, and we questioned her about it. I suppose she felt she was caught red-handed and confessed, demanding we tell no one."

Mrs. Thomas could stand no more. She rose from the swing with all the dignity she could muster, drew a deep breath, and with head held high, she marched into the house and up the stairs. *For the life of me I can't understand how all this happened. Didn't Hattie and I enjoy a special moment yesterday? Didn't we offer a sincere prayer together? How can things be so good and then turn bad in such a short time?*

Reaching her room, Mrs. Thomas fell into her chair and grabbed a cushion to cover her face and muffle her sobs.

Time evaporated as she questioned all that had happened. *How can this be? Is there nothing I can believe in anymore? Is there no help from praying or trusting in God? Does He really hear people when they pray?*

The hurt inside her became intolerable; she grabbed her attic Bible and opened it defiantly. Feeling betrayed, she looked at the words. Her eyes puffed from crying, she could barely make out the words at first. Then the passage cleared and she saw, "Trust in the Lord with all thy might and lean not to thy own understanding."

Mrs. Thomas wept new tears, wondering what good it would do to trust now. The awful thing had already happened! She gave way to utter dismay, and her cries became wails of disbelief and lost hope. Engrossed in her despair, she barely heard a faint knock. Her eyes brimmed in tears as she opened the door.

Standing in the hall was Kate. Tears trailed down her cheeks. "May I come in and talk with you, Mrs. Thomas?"

She had no reason to say "no," so she nodded her head and stepped aside to allow Kate to enter her room.

"I'm not much into company now, Kate, but I can tell you are wrought up over something. What is it?"

Kate dragged herself to a chair to delay what she was determined to tell. "Oh, Mrs. Thomas, this is so hard and I'm not sure I should tell it." She jerked straight up in the chair and blurted out, "Hattie is here, in my room!"

Mrs. Thomas was speechless, struggling to grasp what she had heard. "Are you telling me, Kate, that Hattie is here, at this minute, in your room?"

"Yes, she is. I was supposed to keep quiet and not tell anyone. Now I have broken my promise. Some friend I am. How can anyone trust me again?" Here Kate broke down again and wailed her discomfort.

"Suppose you start at the beginning and tell me what in the world is taking place around here!" Mrs. Thomas sat in her chair, feeling her emotions reaching their limit.

"It all started when Charlie came back and wanted to talk with Hattie. You remember—they went for a walk. It seems Charlie did a good talk job on Hattie. He wanted her to go away with him and be married the next day."

Kate paused and debated in her mind whether she should continue. In a rush of words, she began again. "Well, Hattie agreed. You know how crazy she is about him. I can see how she would feel that way—he is so attentive to her. I'm sure you noticed it too. Well, she mentioned the daughter and asked about her, asking how she would take to her father getting married. He somehow soothed her fears away."

"Kate, would you go ask Hattie to come see me? I don't see how I can help her, but I'd like to try."

While Kate was gone, Mrs. Thomas bowed her head and prayed fervently for help and guidance for both Hattie and herself. She believed what they had shared on the previous day had been real, so how could things have gone so wrong so quickly? Could people fool themselves into thinking they had experienced something special when they hadn't?

The door opened and Hattie flew into Mrs. Thomas's arms. Her sobs crowded out any attempt to talk. Mrs. Thomas could not hold back—she joined Hattie in sorrow by adding her own groans and tears.

Dusk projected a shadow in the room when Hattie lifted her head and spoke. "I'm so sorry, Mrs. Thomas. How can I ask you to forgive me when I made a choice that was so wrong? I didn't feel right when I went off with Charlie. I did protest several times. Then I was swayed by his charm and made an awful mistake."

"Hattie, why did you leave? And where in the world did you go after you left here? Goodness, girl, what a fright we had."

"I packed my belongings into my satchel before I left this morning. Charlie came by to pick me up when I left work. We rode his buggy to his home in Bloomington. He said his mother and Hannah were there waiting for us. There was someone waiting for us all right—his wife!"

Through her tears, she finished telling Mrs. Thomas what happened when they got to Charlie's house. It seems Charlie was surprised to see his wife. He called her Rose and asked what she was doing there.

"I ran from the house to a store on the corner. I told the clerk I needed a way home and asked if she knew of someone. I waited in the store for about a half hour, scared to death that Charlie would come looking for me. Finally, there was a family heading to Ellettsville with a load of stone."

"Why didn't you let me know when you returned, dear child? I was at my wit's end." She still was at her wit's end!

"I was too ashamed and planned to leave as soon as I found a place I could stay. I asked Kate not to let anyone know. I failed you, and I failed myself. I've always been afraid of my shadow, and then I end up doing something like this!"

"Now, Hattie. It's all over and no harm has come to you. Let's be thankful you are home. That attic Bible says that we have all sinned and fallen short of God's glory, so you have a lot of company. Now we'll pray and thank Him that you are home safe."

After they prayed, Hattie went to her room to cuddle in her own bed. Mrs. Thomas sat deep in thought. How close they had come to deep trouble. But it ended well and for that, she was thankful. She prayed she would not again be guilty of doubt.

She crawled into her bed and pulled her grandmother's quilt up to her chin. She was ready to leave the troubles of the day behind.

It was morning. Mrs. Thomas walked down toward the mill, longing to hear the whistling and clacking of the old Monon. As she neared the mill, she saw Mrs. Lang coming toward her.

Mrs. Thomas determined to find out what Mrs. Lang had done with that nine hundred dollars. They greeted each other with warm hugs.

Mrs. Thomas didn't take time to make polite conversation. "Mrs. Lang, I've been dying to know what in the world you did with the nine hundred dollars you found under the floorboards."

Mrs. Lang laughed and recounted the story. "Well, the first thing the girls and I did was to dance around in circles. We laughed and had a big time. That woke up our little fella, so we danced again and he joined as best he could—mostly by sittin' on the floor, grinning and clapping his little hands.

"But what did you do with the money?" Mrs. Thomas's nerves were taut.

"Well, after we settled down some, we each gave our thoughts on what to do with it. Then after we agreed on a plan, the girls and the little fella and I started to town to fulfill our mission. We went into the . . ."

Mrs. Thomas heard a loud noise and looked around to see what it was. Blurred images began to come into focus, and there on the nightstand was her alarm clock sounding its morning alarm. Mrs. Thomas was upset about missing the rest of Mrs. Lang's story and slammed the alarm off a little harder than she should have. Even if it was a dream, she might have learned where that money was!

Then she felt ashamed of her childish behavior and whispered a prayer to be forgiven. *That refining business is sure hard on the flesh!* She scurried around to get ready for the day.

ॐ

Mrs. Thomas's thoughts wandered and she returned to her reminiscing about meeting Elmo. She enjoyed just thinking of that memory. After washing and dressing, she had sat and waited for him to return. He finally did. He picked up her muddy clothing and said, "Come on."

When they got back to where the wagon had been, it was gone. Elmo and the wagon man had moved everything to her house and placed it on the porch. They had even wiped the furniture clean. That improved her spirits somewhat.

Elmo told Mrs. Thomas to sit in a chair, and the two men began to carry her furniture inside. What caught her attention then was that brown dog. She was still angry with him! As she watched him, he slipped away, nearly on his stomach, with his eyes fixed on her. When he reached a safe distance away from her, he lay down slowly. Placing his head between his paws, he continued to stare at her. She had never seen such sorrowful eyes. Whenever Mrs. Thomas made a move, the dog looked ready to run.

After a while, she couldn't take it any longer. She had all she could stand of those mournful looks. She actually began to feel sorry for the dog. Placing her hands in her lap in a nonaggressive way, she softly called, "Here, boy." She did not know a dog could move so fast. He plopped himself at her feet and looked up at her. She was sure his eyes said, "Thanks." Then, nuzzling closer, he quickly fell asleep. A new and lasting friendship had been formed.

Mrs. Thomas returned with a start to the present as the girls came rushing into the dining room for breakfast. She glanced at Elma and saw signs of late night crying. Well, Mrs. Thomas never held a grudge, and she held none against this girl. When Elma was ready to talk, Mrs. Thomas would help her any way she could.

Hattie was subdued and ate silently without offering conversation. Kate and Mandy spoke only to ask for the salt and pepper to be passed. Mrs. Thomas kept herself busy, trying not to be overcome by the tension in the room.

Chapter 8

After breakfast, the women gathered on the front porch. The morning mealtime had been quiet. Even now, no one wanted to say a word, and the tension seemed to build. Mrs. Thomas felt she must break the silence to ease the atmosphere.

"Did you girls hear what happened to Mr. Lang after the ruckus with Elmo and old Trix? I tell you, that man may have been a pain to Mrs. Lang, but he has spiced up my life!" She waited for someone to ask about Mr. Lang. No one did, so she started her story. "It's a shame you missed old Trix hangin' on to the mister's blanket and pulling it off. Seems as though Mr. Lang would start to wear his clothes, all the times he's been exposed in his long johns! If Elmo hadn't called Trix off, there's no telling what might have happened."

Silence prevailed after Mrs. Thomas ended her saga. Everyone's thoughts were occupied elsewhere.

Elma sighed and leaned forward. "The way I see it, Charlie made a fool out of you, Hattie. He turned on his charm with a smile and a soft voice, and you swallowed it hook, line, and sinker. I didn't trust him from the start."

Tension grew. The group held their breath, all wondering how Elma could be so bold. They waited for Hattie to blow up and follow with her personal brand of wailing.

However, tears ran down Hattie's face as she calmly answered. "I know I jumped at the chance to be with Charlie. I understand why you blame me. Just let me explain my thoughts and feelings. Then you might be less harsh in your judgment of me."

The ladies feared the fur would start to fly and glanced at Elma to see her reaction. Surprisingly, she leaned back and looked down at her feet.

Hattie composed herself and started her revealing self-analysis. "You don't understand. My life has not been a happy venture. As I was growing up, I was teased until I cried; then I was teased more. The more I cried, the more I was teased. The boys mocked my name and made rhymes about it. Hattie, fatty, batty.

At that, the ladies laughed and couldn't stop. Finally, Hattie joined in the tittering. Their laughter was so loud, they missed hearing Elmo approach. Old Trix ran up and joyfully greeted the ladies.

Elmo's voice rang out. "It sounds like the silly farm here today. Maybe I need to come back when everyone is happy!" The laugher gradually subsided. He smiled and told them he had dropped by to fix the screen door.

It was clear the rest of Hattie's story would have to wait, and the ladies wandered off. Hattie looked happier, at least. Mrs. Thomas remained on the porch swing to watch Elmo mend the squeaky screen door.

"Well, Anna, what was the outburst of laughter I heard as I rode up? It excited Trix so much he jumped out of the wagon and ran up to join in the fun."

Mrs. Thomas reached out and rubbed Trix's ears as she debated how much to reveal to Elmo. She decided to fill him in.

Elmo worked on the screen door as Mrs. Thomas related the story to him. He got upset hearing how the name rhyming hurt Hattie. He told his own story of how he endured the same kind of teasing when he was young. Elmo said his names were smellmo, tellmo, and bellmo. Mrs. Thomas and Elmo laughed so hard they couldn't get their breath.

Later they sat in the swing and enjoyed the sounds of the morning. Old Trix lay at the feet of the person he loved, pleased when she rubbed his ears from time to time. Peace prevailed on the porch. Even the breeze made a musical sound as it blew gently around the corner of the house.

"Wonder what makes some people want to say and do mean things, Annie?"

"I can give you the reason for many things, Elmo, but for the life of me, I don't know how being mean can help anyone. It beats me."

"This is a pleasant mornin', Annie, and I'm glad I decided to stop over. 'Course, my work is getting' ahead of me since I've been spending so much time over here."

"Why, Elmo Martin, I have a good mind to send you packin' for home." As they enjoyed the moment, Charlie walked up the path.

Elmo tensed up, and Mrs. Thomas shifted nervously in the swing. Trix started to growl when he sensed the uneasy mood in the air. Elmo told him to lie still and be quiet. He obeyed, but the hair on his back stood straight up, and he growled softly.

Charlie reached the porch and greeted Elmo and Mrs. Thomas. He shocked them with his next words: "May I speak to Hattie, please?"

Mrs. Thomas's lips moved, but no words came from them. Looking at her, Elmo realized it was up to him to respond. He stood and faced the young man.

"I have no authority here, Charlie. However, I doubt if Hattie wants to see you—now or ever."

"You must understand I can't leave until I discuss some things with her. Please ask her and let her decide."

Elmo glanced at Annie to see if she wanted to respond. *Hmmm. This must be what Lot's wife looked like.*

Hattie walked slowly out onto the porch. She didn't say a word—she just looked at Charlie.

Elmo could see everything was in his hands. Hattie was almost as unresponsive as Annie. "Charlie, I said I have no authority here, but I advise you to stay in full sight of Trix and me." Trix growled his agreement.

Hattie slowly approached Charlie and they plodded down the path together. She still looked as though she was in shock. Charlie guided, holding her elbow.

Elmo sat back down by Mrs. Thomas. He glanced at her and noted her color was better. He gave her a gentle shake and asked how she felt. She took a deep breath and muttered, "If I live to be a hundred years old, I will never forget this day. What in the world is he doing here? I am surprised she is walking with him. If that don't beat all!"

"Annie, I think you'd better sit back and take a deep breath. You are beside yourself." She realized Elmo was right and leaned back, breathed deeply, and began pushing the swing in a slow rhythm.

Suddenly Mrs. Thomas jumped up and pulled open the screen door, declaring she had to get some nourishment." I feel as if I've been pulling weeds in the garden all day!"

Elmo sat in the swing and wondered what Hattie and Charlie were discussing. They sure looked tense. Charlie did the talking, wildly gesturing with his hands.

Mrs. Thomas returned to the porch and handed Elmo a sandwich and a glass of lemonade.

"This is a welcome treat, Annie. I admit this morning has worn me out too!"

"Have you any idea what is going on out there, Elmo? I don't see any hope from that situation. Do you?"

"Annie, you are the one with the foresight. I must say you are right ninety percent of the time too!"

"Mrs. Thomas laughed at that. "My land, Elmo. That's only women's intuition at work."

No sooner had she made that statement than she saw Hattie and Charlie turn and start back to the house. Her heart beat a hole in her chest, or so it seemed. She wondered what was next.

It did not take long to learn. Charlie walked up the steps almost defiantly and addressed Mrs. Thomas. "I will return here this evening, and Hattie will leave with me. She and I will be married, as was planned. We have decided between us that this is what we want to do. No one else needs to worry further."

Hattie did not look distressed. In fact, she looked content. Did Charlie have a power over her she couldn't overcome? Could he have threatened her if she refused to go with him? Whatever it was, Hattie looked like the cat that ate the canary!

Mrs. Thomas wondered if she should say something just in case Charlie was exerting a power over Hattie. She started to speak to Hattie, but Elmo shook his head at her. *Now why did he do that? He can't read my mind. Even if he could, what right does he have to signal me not to say anything?*

Charlie spoke a word to Hattie, waved his hand, and left. When he was out of sight, Hattie ran into Mrs. Thomas's arms and wailed as only Hattie could do. Between sobs, she tried to tell her story. Mrs. Thomas suggested they sit in the swing. Surprisingly, despite the tears and sobs, Hattie explained the plans she and Charlie had made.

Elmo shook his head in disbelief and declared, "You ladies are either laughing or crying. I've never seen such a bunch! I had better go now before I get mixed up and laugh when I should cry."

Mrs. Thomas waved him off and turned to Hattie. "Do you trust Charlie?"

"Oh, I do. I found it hard to believe he had betrayed me, but I certainly felt yesterday that we were finished. Mrs. Thomas, I prayed so hard to accept it, if that was the way it was to be. But it turns out he has been honest after all. I hardly know where to start. First, I must confess my wrong. The other night, Charlie told me he wanted us to be married. He also said he would come by and pick me up after work yesterday. I packed my clothing, planning on going away with him."

"Did Charlie ask you to run off with him?"

"He said he wanted to get married, and he would stop to pick me up after work. I surmised the rest myself. But don't you see? I was willing to do it. To sneak off with him like that. Now I am so ashamed."

"Hattie, now is the time to make it right. Kneel down at the swing. Confess your sorrow for a wrong choice and ask to be forgiven. It will truly lift the load."

Mrs. Thomas bowed her head to add her prayer as Hattie fell to her knees and cried out her sorrow and her guilt. She stood, and it was obvious her burden had been lifted. Her face glowed as she hugged Mrs. Thomas.

"Hattie, how could Charlie explain away what happened when you arrived at his house?"

"It is tricky, I will admit. When we walked in, no one else was there, but I had no reason to worry. I expected Hannah to appear any time because I heard a noise in another part of the house. Then, without warning, the door flew open and a wild woman dashed in screaming she was Charlie's wife and how could he bring another woman into their home."

Hattie's face reflected the terror of that moment. She composed herself and continued. "I took off then, as I mentioned, and waited at the store for a ride home. Today Charlie told me the whole story. The noise I heard in the house was the minister's wife preparing a wedding meal. Here comes the scary part. The wild woman is Rose, a former friend of Charlie's. She wanted more than friendship and hung around for nearly a year. She even spoke of marriage. Charlie did want to find a good mother for Hannah, as well as a wife for himself."

"He held back because he wasn't sure about her, is that it?" Mrs. Thomas began to understand things clearly.

"That's exactly it. You are sharp, Mrs. Thomas. He tried to be kind and not hurt her feelings, to no avail. In her mind, she thought she just had to wait and Charlie would come around. She spent some time with Hannah. When Charlie was around, she was the picture of kindness to his daughter. But gradually Charlie developed an uncomfortable feeling because of the way Hannah responded to Rose. One day Hannah showed him a bruise on her arm. Rose had warned Hannah to keep it secret, or she would take Hannah's daddy far away from her."

"It is plain to see now why Hannah didn't want to have anything to do with you, Hattie. My word, I'm afraid I misjudged that little girl too! It is clear to me why the attic Bible says not to judge. We don't know all the facts."

"Anyhow, the reason Charlie didn't settle this sooner is that he had to take care of things with the constable. By the way, he got a glimpse of Mr. Lang when he was in the constable's office. He was sweeping out the jail and doing other jail duties. Charlie said he looked happy."

Mrs. Thomas wondered how he could look happy when he had lost nine hundred dollars! *Was Mr. Lang wondering where that nine hundred went? I still wonder what Mrs. Lang did with that money!*

"Well, back to your story, Hattie. That is a lesson for all. Don't hurry into marriage. Take time and make sure it's right."

"I am glad Charlie took time, that's a fact. Otherwise, there wouldn't be a Charlie and me!"

Mrs. Thomas hugged Hattie. It was the end of a nightmare. She breathed a silent prayer that everything would work out for Charlie and Hattie.

The sound of talking and laughing from the girls walking up the path brought the realization that it was lunchtime, with no food on the table. Mrs. Thomas jumped to her feet and rushed into the house. She had chicken and dumplings, but it was meant for supper. However, she would cross that bridge when she came to it!

Elma walked in with Kate and Mandy following. They greeted her and then went up to their rooms to wash for lunch. *I'm so eager to tell everyone the good news, but there will be no time at lunch.* However, the tale will provide a lovely evening on the porch swing after supper. The thought gave her a wonderful feeling. Mrs. Thomas couldn't wait to tell them about Hattie and Charlie.

Chapter 9

It was finally suppertime. Mrs. Thomas had waited as long as she could—she had to tell the girls the news about Hattie and Charles! As soon as their plates were filled and the dining room became quiet, Mrs. Thomas cleared her throat. The ladies knew this was story time and braced themselves for the inevitable.

Elma certainly didn't want to miss another meal. She considered her choices: Should she eat slowly and endure the story or gulp her food and get out fast.

Kate and Mandy sat like two frogs on a log and cast glances at each another. What one did, the other always followed—although their approaches differed. Kate always considered her thoughts before she spoke—she didn't want to hurt anyone. However, Mandy didn't share Kate's kind spirit. Mandy was outspoken and didn't much care what other people thought.

Hattie was not at the dinner table. She was fervently packing her worldly possessions into valises and boxes, filling them to the brim. Charlie would return soon with a borrowed wagon to take Hattie to her marriage and her new home.

Mrs. Thomas felt the time was right to entertain the girls with her Hattie tale and tell them they had a wedding to attend later that evening. She cleared her throat again and noted the girls repositioned themselves. She was positive it was because they were eager to hear her story.

"We misjudged Charlie, girls. He wanted Hattie to marry him, and he took her to his house. She thought his mother and Hannah would be there, but they weren't. Hattie ran when she saw the supposed wife. Charlie was calling for her to wait and let him explain. Hattie didn't see the minister's wife rush from the kitchen to stop the screaming woman from pounding Charlie."

"The wedding was to take place in Charlie's home, and the minister's wife was preparing a light meal. The wild woman is a girl who had attached herself to Charlie—hoping, I suppose, to become his wife. She mistreated Hannah and warned her that if she told anyone, she would be taken away from her daddy."

The ladies listened to Mrs. Thomas relate Hattie's tale despite themselves. She excitedly explained how everything had been resolved and that Hattie was leaving to marry Charlie that very night! The girls were delighted.

Elma thought, *It's not so bad. At least I haven't had to listen to a Lang tale today!* But then Mrs. Thomas cleared her throat— again.

"Goodness, I forgot to tell you girls. Charlie took that woman to the constable's office, and you'll never guess who was there doing yard work. Mr. Lang!"

Kate and Mandy rolled their eyes. Elma jumped up with such haste that she turned over her chair as she rushed out of the room.

Mrs. Thomas watched her leave. "Well, I never. Do you think she choked on my dessert? I worried it might not be sweet enough."

A dog barked and they heard Elmo telling old Trix to calm down. Everyone headed for the door when they heard, "Annie, can you gals give a poor man a hand?"

Old Trix greeted them enthusiastically as they walked out onto the porch. He wiggled and jumped with excitement. When his fervor ebbed a bit, he moved close to Mrs. Thomas. As far as he was concerned, no one else there mattered.

"Sakes alive, Elmo. What are you doing with the wagon?" Mrs. Thomas noticed blankets in the wagon bed.

"Well, my dear lady, I am here to help the soon-to-be-couple move the bride's furnishings to the groom's home. Then after the marriage, I aim to have a shivery for them. Everyone loves that, except maybe the couple." With that, he gave a loud roar and threw back his head to make the most of his laugh.

Mrs. Thomas, her eyes shining, laughed with Elmo and declared it was an excellent idea. "I haven't been to a shivery for years, Elmo. I will get food ready for the folks who come to honor them—at least that's how I see it. More than likely, people will come to tease the young couple. But never mind. As I remember, fun is had by all at a shivery."

Hattie came out the front door with an armload. Elmo walked over to give her a hand placing her things in the wagon. "Lead the way, young lady, and I will finish getting your belongings into the wagon."

After a couple of trips up and down the stairs, all Hattie's belongings were loaded. "I didn't know I had this much stuff. ' Course I have been saving things since I was a young girl. I have pillowcases, scarves, and tablecloths. My mother made many things for my hope chest and I'll finally get to use them." Hattie gave a giggle and dropped her head. She thought, *At last, at last!* Feeling embarrassed, she turned and retreated into the house.

❧

The evening events turned out perfect. No strange woman ran screaming through Charlie's door. Hannah was present and posed no problem. The minister joined in the marriage feast. Hattie and Charlie made a delightful pair—their love for each other was clear. Time came to leave, and all the guests left the newlyweds' home.

After dark, the town's young folks gathered to celebrate the marriage shivery. They circled the house and banged on pans, calling out the newlyweds' names until Charlie and Hattie came outside. Then the cheers started. The couple was placed in a small wagon, and flowers were spread over them. Then the young men pulled them around the town loudly chanting, "Newlyweds, newlyweds!" Some of the townspeople came out to cheer the couple on.

After the parade around town, the couple returned to their home, and Mrs. Thomas served her goodies. After the last crumb was gobbled, and the punch bowl empty, everyone left for home. Mrs. Thomas felt it had indeed been a satisfying shivery. At last, things had worked out for Hattie.

❧

One morning several days later, Mrs. Thomas finished cleaning the kitchen after the breakfast meal was over and the ladies had left for their jobs. The house felt empty to her this morning. She hadn't dreamed how much she would miss Hattie.

Her thoughts wandered to the previous evening. Mandy had remarked that she might get a seat on the swing more often, now that Hattie was gone. Kate told her she could always have her seat. "I'd just as soon sit on the top step with Elma, anyway." Mrs. Thomas thought the ladies seemed to be at loose ends now that Hattie was gone.

Snapping back to the present, she thought, *Well, I have other fish to fry today.* She planned to visit Mrs. Lang. She did wonder what had happened to the nine hundred dollars. She had no plan to meddle in Mrs. Lang's affairs, even if the lady did need help in managing the money. *Well, the poor soul hasn't had a dime her whole life. She wouldn't begin to know how to handle it!* She thought Mrs. Lang was lucky to have a friend like her.

Hurrying from the house, she made her way down the mill road. Although she was intent on learning what Mrs. Lang had done with the money, the real reason she headed that way was to pick up extra baking supplies. She planned to take some baked goodies to Hattie and Charlie.

As she neared the Lang place, Mrs. Thomas could see it looked deserted. Usually there was a chair on the porch or a toy in the yard; she saw no sign of life. That puzzled her, and fear crept into her heart. She ambled on toward the mill.

Two men were working in the first mill building she came to. Mrs. Thomas walked in and voiced her question: "Do you know Mrs. Lang, or do you know where she is? Her house is right across there, but it's empty."

One fellow kept filling his flour sack, but the other put his sack down and said, "It was the funniest thing. Last week a truck backed up to their door, and two men loaded everything from the house into that truck. The rest I can tell you by hearsay. One of the Lang girls came to talk to us, as she had a few times before. She was excited and about to burst. She proclaimed she had a new daddy. We didn't know how to handle that, but

I told her she was lucky to have a new dad. She laughed and told me she had the same daddy, but he was different."

Mrs. Thomas was about to go crazy. "Where is Mrs. Lang?" She knew she sounded too harsh and toned down a little to tell him she was worried.

The fellow pointed to a spot behind her. "If you look over there, I think you will have the answer to your question."

Mrs. Thomas whirled around. There came Mrs. Lang walking toward her. And my, didn't she look grand. Mrs. Thomas didn't think she would have known her had not the mill man pointed her out.

Mrs. Lang walked up to her, a big smile on her face. "I'm glad you are here." She held up an envelope and said she was going to the post office to mail it. "But now all I have to do is hand it to you." She gave it to Mrs. Thomas and explained it would tell her all that had taken place in her life lately. Then she left to meet her husband—they were off to buy new furniture!

Chapter 10

Not willing to read her mail in front of the workers, Mrs. Thomas decided to forget about baking that week. Instead of buying supplies, she scurried home to read the letter. She was so out of breath when she reached the swing, she fell on it. Her legs could not hold her up. Her weakness was caused by not only the hurried walk home, but also anxiety and anticipation. With shaking hands, she tore open the envelope. Two sheets of paper fell out.

Mrs. Thomas,

You have been so kind to me that I feel I should explain what has happened since I last saw you. That day was awful, as we both know, but it is behind me now. James and I have a new life. I will try to explain.

James was charged with disturbing the peace. The constable told him he saw something good in him and had James do work for the town instead of putting him in jail.

Can you believe it? Yes, but here's the catch. He ordered James to attend a camp meeting being held at the edge of town. He had to attend as long as the meeting was in this area.

James said he didn't mind that. He planned to go and lie in the grass and sleep through the services. That's what he did for a week and a half.

Then one night the people attending the service were laughing and crying and hugging one other. He said he could tell by their faces they were happy, and he didn't know why. Suddenly, he was jealous; he wanted to be happy like that too.

James can't explain it, but he said the next thing he knew, he was on the ground and crying in front of all the people. He said he didn't care what they thought. All he cared about was getting rid of hurting and feeling he was no good.

He pleaded with the preacher to tell him what to do. The next thing he knew, there was a Bible in his hand and someone pointed to a page, telling him it was Acts 3:19. After reading the passage, he asked what repent meant. The preacher explained to James that repent means to turn around, to be sorry for the bad things we have done and to stop doing them. He added that the Bible says we have all sinned, and none of us deserve to go to heaven. But Jesus died to pay the penalty for our sin. If we admit we have sinned, accept Jesus and the sacrifice He made, and turn from our old ways, we will belong to God and will go to heaven. One of the first steps we should take after we receive Jesus is to be baptized.

James said he didn't understand much of it, but he did know he was full of sorrow about the mess he had made of his life. He was ready to do whatever it took to get the load off his shoulders.

Several people called saints told him about Jesus going into the water to be baptized. When He came up out of the water, the Holy Spirit hovered over Him in the shape of a dove and a voice was heard from heaven. The Bible said Jesus was filled with the Holy Ghost and went about doing good.

James was so desperate; he said he wanted to do the same thing as Jesus. So he prayed right then and there. He asked Jesus to forgive Him and suddenly felt a peace he had never known. He felt light as a feather!

Then he was baptized and when he came up out of the water, he heard a voice too. It was his voice, but he didn't know what he was saying. James laughed. "I heard my voice and I didn't know what I was saying, but I didn't care, 'cause I was laughing and dancing around with all the rest of them."

That's about it, Mrs. Thomas. I want you to know I am happy. James is taking me to the meetings. I will soon take the step he did. I feel the tugging in my heart.

Oh, by the way, I showed the money to James—I had never spent it. Now we both laugh about that awful day! James explained he had worked some jobs and was saving money to buy a special gun. But we gave part of the money to the preacher to carry on his services. We bought new clothes for all of us and put a down payment on a house. I hope I don't sound too religious if I say, "Thank the Lord from whom all blessings flow!" That's what James says all the time.

Thanks for everything,
Evie Lang

Mrs. Thomas held the letter to her chest and relished the happiness that had come to Evie and Mr. Lang. She wondered,

Is he really that happy? Did the experience really change him that much? Suddenly she felt sad. She wanted to experience that same kind of happiness. Tears began to fall from her eyes, and melancholy enveloped her. How she hated that feeling. Why did she feel that way so often? She wished she could talk about it with someone, but there was no one who could help her. She had never felt more alone.

A rumbling sounded in the lane, and a dog barked. Recognizing the familiar sounds, her spirits rose. She ran into the house to sponge her face—she didn't want Elmo to see she had been crying.

Elmo was sitting in the swing when Mrs. Thomas returned to the porch. "Good morning to you, Annie. How are you this fine day?"

Mrs. Thomas was afraid she was about to cry, so she sat on the swing to compose herself before answering. "Good morning to you, Elmo. The same goes for you, my furry friend." She leaned over to pat Trix and give his ears a rub. Fully satisfied, he plopped down at her feet.

"What are you doing gallivanting about this time of day, Elmo? I hope you aren't looking for food." She laughed and said the ladies were eating lunch at the community building. "I aim to have a beef sandwich with a salad and then a dish of peaches."

"I can tell you, Annie, you talked me into it. In fact, on the way over I said to myself, I hope Annie has beef sandwiches with a salad and follows up with peaches."

"You are about to get your wish, Mr. Martin. Come on in while I get it together."

When the food was on the table, Mrs. Thomas commented, "This is later than I normally eat—I had other things going on this morning."

"Well, let's sit down. You can tell me all about your "other things" as we eat."

"I don't know that I can discuss it, Elmo. I can give it a try, but I doubt it will make sense." Mrs. Thomas was quiet for a spell to clear her thoughts.

"To start out, I get a sadness that comes over me—usually at dusk. Today it came a short time before your arrival. I can't shake the melancholy. If I could figure out the cause, maybe I could get rid it."

"Annie, I'm not a head doctor, but we can talk about it to see if something comes up. Think back to different periods in your life. Begin with your youngest age and work up to the present. Stay on each age for a few seconds to detect any change in emotion. If one age causes discomfort, stay with it and start telling me everything you recall from that time in your life."

Mrs. Thomas leaned back in her chair and silently began following Elmo's suggestion. Elmo sat quietly by as Mrs. Thomas went back in her memory to earlier days. He felt bad about her bouts with melancholy, as she called it. She was a good woman, perhaps a bit nosy—or maybe *interested* would be a better word. He felt that was a problem with most women. On the other hand, to be fair he thought about times the guys had been together discussing different people and what they did or did not do right. He gave a laugh as he thought about those times.

Mrs. Thomas's reverie was broken by Elmo's laugh. "Wha's so funny?" He gave her a smile and shrugged his shoulders.

Mrs. Thomas didn't return to the journey through her memories. She had felt close to a revelation at one time, but moved on, afraid of what she might encounter. She stood, declaring she must clear up the table before time to serve supper. In her hurry, a plate slipped from her hand and crashed to the floor. Without warning, she began to shake and cry. She sank back into the chair and gave way to her tears.

To see Annie crying threw Elmo for a loop. He wasn't sure what move to make. Should he let her cry, or try to comfort her. He had no idea what was causing her to act like this. In his fear of doing the wrong thing, he made no move. However, she knew he was close by and willing to do anything she asked of him.

After what seemed to be a lifetime, the sobbing ended and Annie raised her head. "Elmo, you have lots of knowledge for a man who claims not to be well educated!"

Glad to hear Annie talking again, he smiled at her and shrugged his shoulders, not sure yet how much to say. He decided to let Annie lead the way. It wasn't long before she began talking.

"Elmo, I think I experienced what may be an insight into my melancholy. I felt the emotions I had at six. As the plate slipped from my hand, I saw broken dishes from another time. At the same time, I heard loud angry voices. Then suddenly I felt a deep melancholy sweep over me. A sense of aloneness overwhelmed me. I froze with fear, afraid I would never escape that scene."

"You no doubt suffered a bad blow when you were a child. Those things do influence one for a lifetime, although we may never connect them to our adult life. Annie, I'm so sorry you have carried this burden all your life."

The opportunity for further discussion ended as they heard all the ladies noisily climbing the porch steps and plopping on the swing. The young women laughed and continued a lively conversation started on the way home. Mrs. Thomas and Elmo walked out to join them.

In a conversational lull, Elma nodded to Elmo. "To what do we owe the honor of your presence this day?" Before Elmo could reply, Elma commented that the screen door was not squeakin'.

Elmo faked a grim look and told Elma he had to check the door to make sure she had not messed with it since he fixed it! They had a laugh over that. Elmo had a quick wit and was always ready with a humorous comeback.

Mrs. Thomas spoke up. "Since Elmo is here, why not fill him in on the matter we discussed some weeks back about the girl Kate knew?" She had noticed that Kate looked sad, even as she was carrying on with the girls, and thought this would give her a lift. However, she noted Kate responded to her suggestion with a look of distress. She regretted bringing up the subject, but it was too late to take her words back.

Elmo picked up the conversation. "What, may I ask, did you discuss? Can your friend, the great wizard, be of help?"

The ladies groaned and rolled their eyes at Elmo's remark. Except Kate. Mrs. Thomas wanted to stop further discussion, but the wheels were already in motion. Elmo asked Elma to start the story since she was the "wise one." "Fill me in on the details, and I'll try to come up with a solution."

"I think Kate needs to tell the tale—it was her friend," Elma responded.

Mandy saw distress on Kate's face and couldn't understand why. Normally, Mandy thought only of herself, but she and Kate were close—even though complete opposites. To help Kate, she offered to tell the tale.

"It started out with when Hattie went with Charlie. Mrs. Thomas was trying to learn where she was, and everyone was afraid to say a word. Hattie had made us promise to keep her secret."

"It was the same day you took Mr. Lang away." Elma's comment caused twitters at the memory of that day. Poor Mr. Lang and his baggy long johns—exposed by a dog!

"Well, anyway," Mandy continued, "I said you have to watch out for the silent ones, meaning Hattie. That prompted Mrs. Thomas to lecture me on judging." Mandy paused and seemed unwilling to say more.

Kate jumped in to explain. "Just because all the facts point to guilt doesn't mean guilty. Mandy thought Hattie was manipulating Mrs. Thomas to get in her good graces. But Mrs. Thomas told us about the dangers of judging someone when we don't know all the circumstances. I told of a girl who was accused of stealing a classmate's money. The evidence was strong. However, I knew she didn't steal the money and said so."

Elmo asked Kate to tell him the story with all the details she remembered. Kate began with the telling. As she got into the story, she was passionate, wanting to prove to all that the girl had been innocent.

When Kate finished her story, Elmo sat back without a word and pondered what she had said. The truth of the story was clear to him, and he felt something he hadn't felt in a long time—heartbreak for someone else. He asked Kate to sit next to him. Sitting down, she looked at Elmo. Her expression reflected fear, sadness, and curiosity about what was next. Looking her full in the face, he reached out and grabbed her hand.

Mrs. Thomas and the ladies sat quiet and looked at Elmo with a questioning look similar to Kate's.

Elmo spoke then, his voice soft and quiet. He gently squeezed Kate's hand. "Kate, you dear girl, to know a truth and to have it disbelieved by all others has been a heavy load for you to carry. You alone know the truth because it is your story. You were accused of stealing a classmate's money, and the shame and hurt have been a thorn in your heart to this day."

Without warning, Kate's face took on the shame and the disgrace she felt. There was something else as well. It was the anger that had festered for years in her heart. She felt chained to the guilt while her accuser went free.

Then she crumbled and seemed to diminish in size by half. Her face changed to grief. She rested her head on Elmo's shoulder, and her tears fell in torrents on his shirt. He put comforting arms around her. Tears fell from the others' eyes as well, as they watched the event play out before their eyes.

The incident that occurred next caused audible sobs from the observers. Trix, who never left Mrs. Thomas's side, got up slowly and silently and went to Kate. He put his head on her lap and stared mournfully at Elmo.

They remained silent, waiting for healing to take place for all of them. Trix knew it was a special a time also. He carefully moved from time to time, but only to change his position.

Kate rose suddenly. She thanked them for helping her and for caring about her. She petted Trix on the head. "I thank you too, dear friend." Trix took that as a release of duty and quickly returned to Mrs. Thomas's feet.

Elmo called Trix, saying it was long past time to get home. As he walked down the porch steps, he turned to Kate and gave her a suggestion that gave no end of pleasure to Mrs. Thomas.

"Kate, I say that later this evening or tomorrow you get together with Annie and have a talk. She can help you a lot. She reads that attic Bible faithfully. It will help! Good night, all."

And he was gone. Following his master, old Trix gave one last glance at Mrs. Thomas.

Chapter 11

Fall was in the air. Flowers were fading. The leaves on the oak trees and ash trees no longer tried to hold on—they gave in to nature and drifted slowly to the ground as they lost their grip. The grass no longer cared to take nourishment from the earth. Its brown color was a testament to that fact.

Slowly rocking in the porch swing, Mrs. Thomas thought it was the same with life. *We struggle to hold on regardless of the fierce winds or the storms of life. We hold on as the rain beats us down, and we endure the unrelenting heat of the sun. Yet when all is said and done, we end up the way of all life.*

She felt wrong thinking those thoughts, but wasn't it true? She used herself as an example. Hadn't she weathered all life handed her? She couldn't count the times she determined to try harder to overcome the obstacles in her life.

That was another thing. No one knew about the rough times she had experienced. Why would they? She kept things to herself. It would be a violation if she revealed her personal feelings to others. She learned that lesson well during her childhood. She remembered how close she had come to revealing herself to Elmo. Why would she want him to learn of her rough times?

Oh sure, she said her calling was to help others. But how could she benefit anyone else when her own life was a series of melancholy episodes? She continued to read her attic Bible and to pray. God was her last and only hope, and she knew it.

Mrs. Thomas wondered if she measured up. No matter how much she read the Bible, she had still had melancholy. She did believe in prayer—she knew she did. So it must mean she didn't measure up. She had read about that in a Bible verse. Wondering how one measures up, she rose to go back into the house and do some busywork before she got depressed again.

She was almost to the screen door when she saw Elmo coming down the lane. There was old Trix jumping and doing circles in the wagon bed, eager to greet her. Never had Mrs. Thomas been so happy to see them, but she wanted to be careful and not let on that anything was wrong.

"Goodness, what a welcome sight! Well, at least Trix," Mrs. Thomas teased. What happened next unnerved her to the bone.

Trix ran up to her and leaned against her leg. He looked up at her and whined a low mournful sound. How was it that she could not fool Trix? How could he sense she had faked her cheerful greeting? She looked at Trix rubbing his head against her leg and heard him emitting a sound that expressed affection and concern. He looked her direct in the eyes as he communicated his love to her in the only way he knew how.

Not able to bear it any longer, Mrs. Thomas dropped to the ground and threw her arms about Trix's neck. She buried her face in his coat, and the floodgates of her grief flowed into his fur. Old Trix was faithful to his post—he never moved, except to rub his face against her neck to let her know he shared her grief.

After a long space of time, Mrs. Thomas kissed Trix and thanked him for the love and the comfort he had given her. It might sound funny to others, but while she was grieving, she thanked the Lord for Trix. Did that sound disrespectful? Well, she did not mean it that way. In her heart, she felt God understood. A verse from her morning Bible reading came to her mind, confirming how she felt. "In all thy ways acknowledge him and he will direct your paths." That was clear enough. She certainly was desperate for direction out of this melancholy.

Elmo had been standing quietly by as the drama unfolded before his eyes. He knew he was outside that moment of time—it involved only Trix and Annie. Then he noticed Annie glancing his way.

"Elmo, I am sorry if I caused a scene. I don't know what came over me. No, Elmo, that is not true. I do know the whole reason. Do you have time to sit awhile and listen to my tale of woe?"

"Now, Annie, you know you have all my time and both my ears. I know I am second best to Trix, but someone has to be the loser." He and Mrs. Thomas settled themselves on the swing. Of course, Trix picked his favorite spot near Mrs. Thomas.

"All right, Annie. The floor—I mean the porch—is yours. Let's hear what is bothering the nicest lady I know."

Mrs. Thomas drew in a deep breath and braced herself. Could she discuss personal things? Elmo sensed the struggle and sat motionless. It was her battle, and only she could decide. Finally, she began.

"You saw the reaction I had when I dropped the glass last summer? Remember, we had started a conversation that we didn't finish because the ladies returned home from work just then. Well, when I dropped the glass, a disturbing vapor filled my mind. I saw myself as a six-year-old again. My mother and I were in the kitchen. She was washing the dishes and I was drying them. Truth be told, I thought I was helping, although I only dried one glass. As I dried the glass, it slipped from my hand and crashed to the floor."

"My father returned home from work at that moment and saw the shattered glass. He began to yell about how hard he worked. Why did he have to have a daughter who didn't take care of things? He said if I had to work for a living, he bet I would be careful then."

"My mother sent me to the cellar, as she always did when my father yelled. She would ask me to get some apples or carrots—anything to get me out of the situation. In later years, I realized she was trying to protect me. It didn't work. Nothing could blot out the sound of my father yelling at me."

Elmo saw the trembling of her body as she relived the scene. Mrs. Thomas continued, her voice betraying the deep emotion she was experiencing.

"After the glass incident, I begin having bouts of melancholy— usually at dusk. Then it began bothering me at other times, as well."

Mrs. Thomas gave a start. "I just realized something. My father didn't yell at other times—it was only when he came home from work—at dusk."

"Sometimes we had fun together. I remember he made a stick doll for me. Occasionally he took me sledding. He worked hard. I noticed his worn shoes and wondered why he didn't get some nicer ones."

"He worked in the Bloomington Stone Mill from dawn to dusk. It don't make it right, but I understand it now. He wasn't angry with me. His anger was aimed at conditions he couldn't make better." Mrs. Thomas wept quietly.

Elmo patted her hand but said nothing. He knew it best to let the tears mend her heart. Trix didn't like her tears and pushed his nose under her hand. He got his ears rubbed as a reward.

"Annie, I'm glad you trusted me enough to share your story. I know how hard it was for you. I'd like to hear about the Monon someday. You mentioned how it comforted you when you heard the train whistle and saw the old train coming down the tracks." Elmo placed his hand on hers.

After Mrs. Thomas wept all her tears, she straightened up and declared it was time for a treat. "I won't rub your ears as I do for Trix, but I do thank you. You are indeed a friend." She hurried into the house to fix them each a generous serving of chocolate cake with a dollop of whipped cream. She would have to send Elmo to the springhouse to get the cream to whip.

She had thought the evening would be lonely with the ladies attending a church event, but it had turned into a delightful time. Elmo was good company. He knew many people and could tell some interesting—and hilarious—stories. They enjoyed the time together.

Maybe she could ask him to take her over to Ellettsville to visit with Lela sometime. She thought about the young woman often. Lela had been one of her first boarders. She tried to think how many years ago it had been since Lela had married and moved away. At least five.

Elmo brought in the cream and said he was going for a short walk with Trix. Turning her thoughts away from Lela, she beat the cream to stiff peaks and folded in the sugar. She hoped Elmo wouldn't be too long—the whipped cream tasted so good!

❧

Mrs. Thomas felt a growing concern. Elmo had left some time before and still she saw no sign of him. Looking out the window, she did see the ladies coming back from their church event. They were walking fast. They all looked glum, and she hoped there hadn't been a disagreement among them. Mrs. Thomas didn't want anything else to worry about. She suddenly felt uncomfortable.

Elma came in alone, which was strange. Where were the rest of the girls? Why were they staying outside? Before Mrs. Thomas could ask a question, Elma burst out loudly. "Mrs. Thomas, I don't know how to say this except to say it. Trix got hurt!"

Mrs. Thomas dropped in a chair and couldn't get her breath. Elma called the other ladies in to help her. Kate wiped her face with a wet cloth, and Mandy fanned her furiously. After a few minutes, Mrs. Thomas came around. Trembling, she asked what had happened. She wanted to know where Elmo and Trix were.

Elma continued, "We were coming out of the community building and saw Elmo walkin' into town carrying Trix. Elmo's face looked awful. We asked him what happened. He shook his head and asked us to tell you he would be back later. He said to have coffee ready."

The girls' faces told the whole story. What they saw of Trix must have been horrible. Mrs. Thomas covered her face with her hands—she didn't know if she could bear to hear more, but she wanted to know the truth.

Elma signaled to someone else to tell Mrs. Thomas the rest. Mandy Jayne felt it was up to her to finish in a way that would be easier on Mrs. Thomas, if that was even possible. "Mrs. Thomas, Trix was just hanging in Elmo's arms and not moving. There was blood all over his legs and on his chest. The blood was dripping on Elmo's clothes and onto the ground." At that, Mandy lost her calm and begin in cry in gulps, unable to say more.

Mrs. Thomas was about to faint with sickness and fear. Elma noticed and asked Kate to hang onto an arm. They guided her toward the bedroom steps. But Mrs. Thomas dug in her heels and stated with sharp, concise words that she wanted to sit on the porch. As they eased her onto the swing, she announced, "I will sit here until Elmo returns. I would be much obliged if one of you would put on the coffeepot."

There she sat, staring into space. She looked like a stone statue and didn't appear even to breathe! Kate sat quietly in the swing next to her.

The night turned dark and chilly. Mrs. Thomas neither moved nor spoke. Kate was afraid to move. She was scared, cold, and felt so tense she could hardly sit there. This was a nightmare. She wondered how it would end.

Then out of nowhere, Elmo appeared by the swing. Mrs. Thomas jumped out of the swing. She grabbed Elmo's arm and in a voice not her own cried out to him, "Don't say the words—just look at me. Is he . . . ?" She could say no more and collapsed on the swing in utter despair.

That was more than Elmo could bear. "Annie, listen. You must be strong and help me bear this. I don't know how this all came about. We started out and Trix was runnin' in front of me. He hit a low spot and tumbled off the path and down an embankment. I lost sight of him for a minute."

Elmo paused as he tried to regain his composure. "Then I heard him whinin' and cryin'. I knew by the sound he was hurt bad. When I got to him, I saw he had tripped an animal trap. It caught his front legs and the tip of his nose. Blood was flowing all over. I tried to release him, but the trap was too strong. Finally, out of desperation, I gave one last heave and the trap released Trix.

Elmo was drained mentally and physically. The color had left his face. Even though the evening was cool, sweat lined his forehead. "Trix was in such pain, and it was even worse when I tried to lift him. But I had no choice—I had to get him to town. He had lost too much blood and he continued to bleed. I had to get him to the doctor—and fast. I didn't think there was much time. I finally got him to Doc Morgan."

Mrs. Thomas cried, "It didn't matter anyway, did it? He's gone jest the same!" Her body sank down into the swing in utter hopelessness.

Elmo went to her and grabbed her hand and sobbed to her, "Annie, listen to me. Trix is alive! He is in bad shape because he lost so much blood, but Doc said he would see what he could do. He doesn't know about his legs and said he would be crippled if he makes . . ." Elmo could no longer bear the thought of losing Trix. " Annie, do you think it would be wrong to pray for Trix?"

The panic in Elmo's voice made Mrs. Thomas ashamed that she had only thought of herself. Still crying, she took his hand.

"Elmo, I don't know why I didn't think about praying for Trix. I have been nothing but self-centered. Please sit down beside me and let's pray for him now."

There sat two heartbroken, believing creatures, crying out to their Creator to heal a dog.

જ

The next day Mrs. Thomas went with Elmo to pay Trix a visit. He heard them and recognized their steps and their voices before they came into sight. They heard him whining and knew he was eager to see them.

He couldn't get up to jump and wiggle, but he thumped his tail on the floor with all his strength. And why shouldn't he? These were the two people he loved more than anything. If he could only get up to greet them!

Mrs. Thomas cried when she saw Trix. It was too much. He hadn't done a bad thing in his life. He always gave his love and comfort fully and unconditionally. How would a dog know how to give comfort, unless it had been instilled in him by a Creator?

Mrs. Thomas laid her head close to his and cried out her sorrow for this good friend. She heard Elmo crying like a baby. Here she was thinking only of herself again.

"Oh. Elmo, remember we prayed for him. Now let's put our faith to work and believe that our dear friend will return to health."

"Yes, Annie, that's what we'll do. We prayed, and now we will trust. They breathed another prayer over Trix before they left. He sensed their calmness and it comforted him. He licked at their hands, as best he could, to show his love. He relaxed then began to fall asleep, soothed by Mrs. Thomas's hand on him and Elmo's quiet breathing. Trix's world was complete.

જ

Mrs. Thomas had to show patience while Trix healed—it was two weeks before he even started to get up and around. However, once he began to improve, he quickly returned to full health—except for one thing. Trix was crippled in his front legs. If he was aware of it, he never let on. He jumped and wiggled as much as before!

Elmo and Mrs. Thomas went for a walk down the lane shortly after Trix returned home. It goes without saying that Trix went with them. When they approached the path that went to Mrs. Thomas's secret place, Trix bolted in ahead of them. Mrs. Thomas and Elmo followed.

When Trix reached the special hiding place, he went to the log where Mrs. Thomas had sat on that day when she had been so upset. Sniffing around, he looked at Mrs. Thomas and wagged his tail.

"Annie, I declare. I think that dog remembers that awful day, and he's showing us how happy he was when he found you."

Mrs. Thomas sat on the same barkless log she had used that day. She threw her arms around old Trix and cried her eyes out with relief and thanksgiving. When her tears subsided, Trix turned toward home. His mission had been accomplished.

Chapter 12

A soft snow was falling as the sun boldly forced a few sparkling rays of light through the kitchen window. Mrs. Thomas sat in her rocker by the crackling fire, enjoying the winter morning.

Her mind strolled through memories of the past year. There had been tears and hurts for herself, as well as for her girls. To think of them even now caused a pain in her heart. But her spirit lightened as she remembered that each painful challenge had brought new understanding of life.

She allowed her mind to take her back to the days when Hattie and Charlie struggled with the problems caused by the old girlfriend. She almost ruined their life before it got started.

One could not forget Hannah. She made Hattie's life miserable for a while! Nevertheless, look how well things worked out for them. The three of them are enjoying life as a loving family.

Her mind drifted to Kate and her heartache. She recalled Kate's story of a friend accused of stealing—but it turned out Kate herself was the "friend"! The painful memories continue to bother Kate, but she could now see how it had appeared to her accuser. Kate is working on true forgiveness. They all learned a lesson from her experience. Mrs. Thomas noticed how everyone, including herself, has tried to avoid judging other people!

She thought of all the things she shared with Elmo last summer. It was only yesterday, wasn't it? It is hard to believe she told him about the melancholy spells. She continued her struggle to overcome those times of depression—but understanding them better has helped.

Mrs. Thomas thought they all learned valuable lessons while going through their heartaches. And she continued to learn from her attic Bible. In fact, thinking of her new discovery made her heart beat faster. In her attic Bible, she read only yesterday how we are to "bear one another's burdens."

It's a two-way thing and requires a willingness to share. How can we bear another's burdens if they don't tell us about them? And how can others help us and pray for us if we aren't willing to share our own burdens? *I think it's clear we shouldn't tramp down the lane and scream our problems, but how sweet it is to confide in dearest friends and family. What relief is found when a burden is shared!* Her greatest comfort came from learning that Jesus bears our burdens.

Mrs. Thomas found tears drifting down her cheeks. She thought of the years she had kept her troubling thoughts secret. Through pride or fear of ridicule, she did not know. Now she truly believed that sharing hurts and problems makes all involved stronger and wiser.

She was eager to share her new knowledge with Elmo when he arrived later that morning. She hoped he would bring Trix with him. Trix was an example of how God thought of us even before we were born. If Mrs. Thomas had created the earth, it's doubtful there would have been dogs. She didn't like them much before she met old Trix. She loved him now, pure and simple. Thoughts of the comfort he brought her last summer made her eyes glisten with tears.

She thought of Elma and Mandy Jayne. She gave a giggle remembering how Mandy hated to be called Mandy Jayne! But the name had stuck nonetheless.

She thought of Elma and the tears she shed most of the late summer—mostly behind closed doors. Well, it would do no good to think about Elma's troubles. She would have to wait until Elma decided to reveal what was troubling her. She had to admit that she was curious though.

Mrs. Thomas considered telling Elmo today what she found so comforting about the Monon and its whistle. But then again, maybe she should wait until spring when they could sit on the swing as she shared her thoughts. She pictured it now and felt the cool breeze on her skin with the warm spring sun fighting to do its part too.

She resolved to get into the present and leave the past, at least for now. However, Mrs. Lang popped into her mind. She couldn't keep from laughing when she thought about Mr. Lang and his long johns. What a sight to see! Evie, as she wanted to be called, had written a letter inviting her to visit them in their new home.

Evie wanted Mrs. Thomas to see what she thought of Mr. Lang's new job. She admitted her curiosity was stirred a bit. However, Mrs. Thomas wanted to see Mr. Lang for other reasons too. Elmo said he would take her to see Evie as soon as all the ice blocks were in the icehouse.

She wanted to ask Mr. Lang about his spiritual experience. Evie said he had changed so much and continued to change. Mrs. Thomas wanted to find out for herself what Mr. Lang did to change so much.

Mrs. Thomas enjoyed the times she could draw Elmo into a Bible discussion—although he usually seemed reluctant. She had learned quite a lot, but knew there was so much more. She longed to add to her understanding.

She jumped up when she heard Elmo's wagon. Peering out the window, she saw him turning into the lane. There was Trix jumping and twisting—his tail thumping Elmo with each wag!

Mrs. Thomas scurried to the door, ready to open it and greet these dear friends. Life was good and she was blessed. No longer was she so foolish to question if prayers would be answered. Aloud she said, "Thank you, Lord, from whom all blessings flow!"

She swung open the door and greeted Elmo warmly with a hug. Then she bent down to greet Trix with a love only they understood.

Look for your favorite friends again in the next book of *Tales from the Front Porch Swing*. See you then!

A personal message to my readers . . .

I hope you've enjoyed the time spent with Mrs. Thomas, Elmo, and all the girls. Personally, I am especially attached to Trix. It's a little sad leaving them now . . . but more *Tales* are on the way!

Thank you for giving me the opportunity to do a work for the Lord. The proceeds from my writings will go to Daniel Barber, a missionary in Brazil who is laboring to help people to a better life through Jesus.

My hope and prayer for each of you is that you are walking with Jesus. If you don't yet have a personal relationship with Him, when you understand the joy and peace that can be yours, I hope you will give Jesus a chance.

> Then Jesus said, "Come to me, all of you who are weary
> and carry heavy burdens, and I will give you rest.
> - Matthew 11:28

We are living in challenging times. No matter what you are facing, Jesus can help you. He doesn't promise to make the problems go away, but He does promise to help us through them.

God created a perfect world—one with no sin and no suffering. But when Adam disobeyed God, sin entered the world, along with pain and problems. God loves us and wants us to live in heaven—a perfect place—with Him forever. But God is holy and cannot allow sin in His presence. To solve this problem, He sent Jesus.

> "For God loved the world so much that he gave his one
> and only Son, so that everyone who believes in him will
> not perish but have eternal life."
> - John 3:16

We have all sinned—done things displeasing to God. The penalty for sin is death. That's what we deserve. But Jesus paid the penalty for us by dying on the cross.

> *For everyone has sinned; we all fall short of God's glorious standard. Yet God, with undeserved kindness, declares that we are righteous. He did this through Christ Jesus when he freed us from the penalty for our sins. For God presented Jesus as the sacrifice for sin. People are made right with God when they believe that Jesus sacrificed his life, shedding his blood.*
>
> - Romans 3:23-25

You don't need to clean up your life to come to Jesus—He will do that for you! Isn't that a bargain? When you accept His gift of life, you will become a new person in Jesus!

Mrs. Thomas is learning about God by reading her attic Bible. That's the best way for you to learn too. You might want to start by reading the Gospel of John in the New Testament. It tells about Jesus. You'll learn that He loves you personally and wants to be your friend.

When you give your life to Jesus, you will forever be changed.

May He bless you,

Iris

Questions? You may contact Iris at IrisWhitney@comcast.net